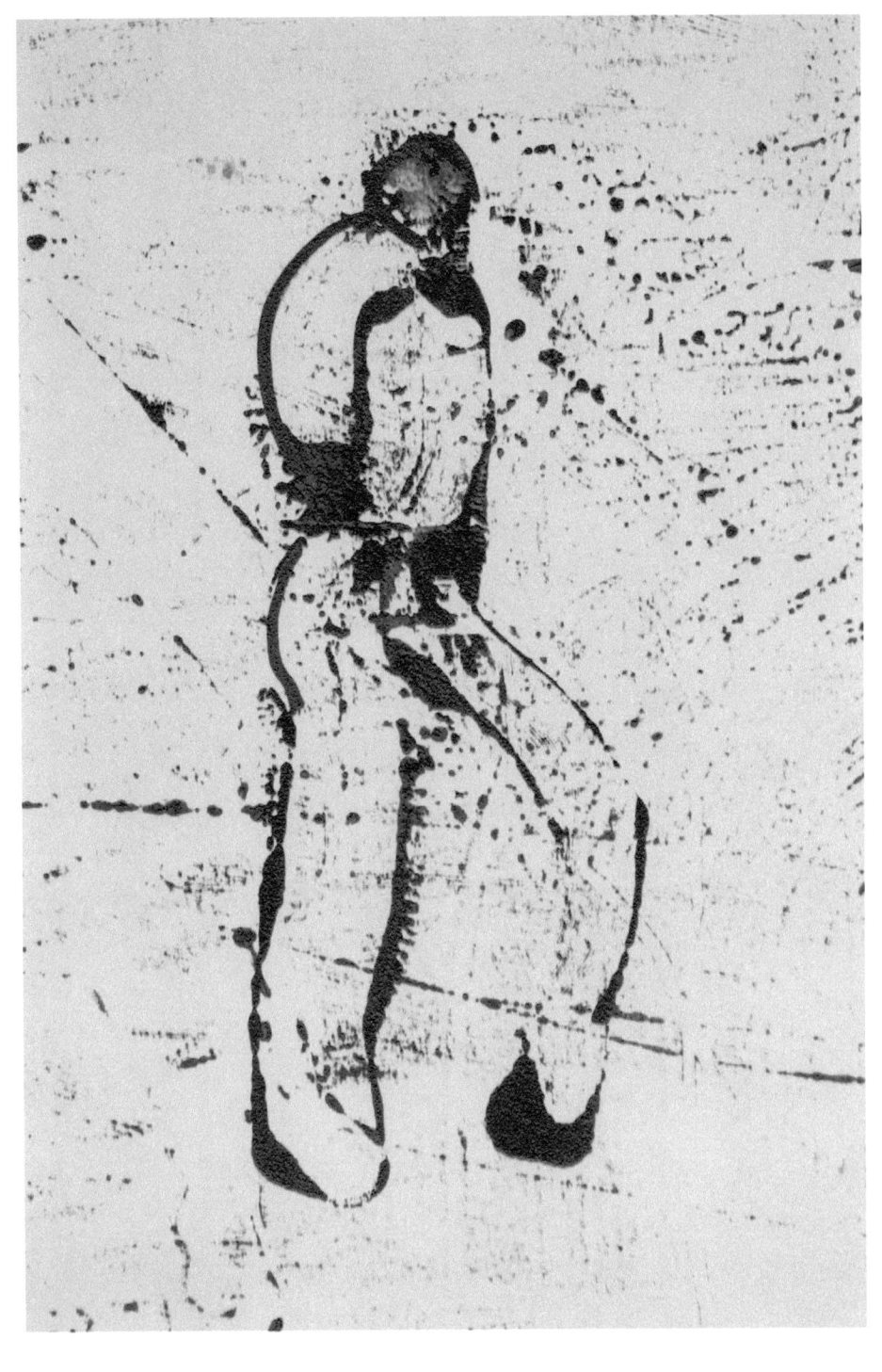

PREVIEW

ORLIN G. OROSCHAKOFF

PREVIEW

Copyright © 2015 by OgoArt

First Createspace Books Edition 2015

ogoart.com

Cover Art by Orlin G. Oroschakoff

Drawing by Orlin G. Oroschakoff

Cambria Type

ISBN-13: 978-0996607506
ISBN-10: 0996607501
LCCN: 2015912270

To Michelle

Fable of Contents

"... it's so easy to write, I wonder why some p – p – people even bother to read," he mutters to himself, seated next to me on my right. We are waiting for the film to start. Quiet and cold inside. Cold and quiet... Did I say that? No, I didn't. I said quiet and cold. That's quite different.

Just two of us in the empty theatre. The big white screen looks way bigger from here. Certainly not straight. Outside, the tramway's wheels are squealing. What wheels...he shifts and presses his moth-eaten colorless hat down onto his unshaven skull.

We are waiting for the previews. Previews my ass. Wrong word. It will press on their urinary tracts. They will run for the bathroom but make sure to be back in time for the main picture (I don't understand why they call it a picture anyway) with more popcorn.

But none of that yet. We stare at the blank screen and wait. How long... Don't know. It's been a while. Waiting is like baiting. Baiting is like waiting. OK...

"No, it's not." He blows at his fingerless wool gloves. "Baiting is like dating. You date – you bait..." He puts his index finger through a hole in his sleeve.

What the fuck... Who the fuck does this guy think he is with his back pressed straight into the back of his seat? His elbow on the armrest of my seat. What is he... Does he think he is Lord Rosse or maybe even Lord Rayleigh occupying the first chair of the first row? I elbow his elbow and regain some territorial advantage. He chuckles...

"What's so funny?" I inquire.

"You."

"How so?"

1

"Clueless."

"Me?"

"Absolutely. I envy you."

"I don't envy you, I just wonder if I should give you a chance to shut up right now or maybe I should box your hairy ear shell into a cauliflower powder."

He turns his dilated pupils towards me. There is some light there inside the entrance, or maybe it's the reflection from the empty screen.

"I haven't discovered the spiral galaxies, not even the inert gas argon – if you wondered – but... your shoelace is untied and worst of all you stink of jazz. That's dangerous." I look down.
He's right. I bend down and while fixing my shoelace I'm confronted by the raw look of his bare feet. The thickly deformed yellowish nail of his fungus-ridden big toe mesmerizes me. Is that a p-phy-sical extension of aesthetic fucking tension?

He reads my mind.

"Could be a writer's sly convention, but it's not. It's the real deal. By the way, it's truly useful for some unrushed existential conclusions. Look at the empty screen – isn't that something? I wish there was a longer delay. Can't stand the movies. Too much movement, noise and color. It's bad. Bad...but things will get worse." He cracks the tips of his long fingers. "Listen... you might wonder why we're seated next to each other while the whole theatre is empty. Wanna know...very simple indeed. It's because we're crossed-outs. I mean obvious ones. You saw the cashier bitch at the ticket booth out there... I said hi to her. She replied, 'Fuck you.' I insisted, 'How are you today?' She gave me a swordfish stare. 'It couldn't be worse.' 'Oh yes... surely it could,' I comforted her. 'One ticket please.' She flipped the blue

2

half of the pencil down and crossed out the first seat on the first row on the right side. Needless to say, the entire ticket chart in front of her was empty. 'Thank you, hon.' I took my ticket. 'Fuck you.' She blessed me once more. A typical encounter between an optimist and a pessimist. Certainly in this social structure, the optimists are the misfits – the 'crossed-outs.' But then... you p-popped out from nowhere. Frothy... isn't it?"

"Fretful, to my estimation." Despite my hangover, I can manage a feeble remark. "The bitch might have expected a huge crowd for this panoramic super-Soviet production... Instead, she gets two fucked-up pariahs."

His stare, still large under heavy lids, drills the powdery blankness of the screen. It seems not to feel time passing.

"What are you doing here?" He cocks his ear and scratches it under the loose end of his earmuffs. Doesn't even wait for an answer. He shoots out the next one, "Why aren't you 'THERE?'"

This itchy, primal need to let loose my left fist to land a compressed left hook on the bridge of his prominent profile creates a conflicting conundrum based on two uncontested pieces of evidence: the poor state of his feet and the eerie resemblance of his profile to my own.

"Why the fuck aren't you THERE?" he insists while his hushed, raspy and low voice examines my hearing at close range. Sober breath.

"Guess why."

"I know why."

"You don't."

"I fucking do"

"You fucking don't."

My cantankerous opponent cracks a pale but combative smile. "I really do."

"Why are you asking me then?"

His bony finger goes in between the unwashed, scuzzy bandage around his neck.

"*Aletheia* – 'what's not forgotten.' The word for Truth in Greek. Truth with a capital T... is basically a form of fiction. I hope you're aware of the fact that fiction is considered untruth. Invented statement or narrative. At least it's p-per-ceived that way by most of the shitheads. A thing feigned or imaginatively invented, THOSE... may even add. Terrible..." his finger interrupts its urgent quest. "In fact, fiction is a conventionally accepted falsehood or pretense..."

"Basically a lie." I meet his pause.

"Yes, basically..."

"That's hilarious."

"No, it's abominable." He finishes his pitch.

"But you didn't tell me why I'm not 'THERE,'" I persist.

He turns his face upward toward the ceiling. "Because..." he makes another point-blank pause. "You are fuckin' HERE." The prolonged immobility of his stiff body considerably increases the ominous broodiness of his statement.

"Look up there. Where the wall and the ceiling meet. There is a live creature there. A big, fat cockroach. Moving slowly, steadily on the upper rim of the electrical bulb. In search of light or warmth one might think... I doubt it. That's a creature designed to deal with dark, slimy sewers, you know. That's p-p-pretty much where the System is p-pushing us and training us to enjoy. But see, the fucking crawler has got a goal. The base of the light bulb. Why? Surely not because of the striking vista from up there, looking down on our heads p-planted over these empty rows of greasy seats. No... Not exactly. The crawling fucker knows p-pre-cisely about the fundamental Truth inside my p-pocket. A slice of stale bread. And boy... isn't he after it. Look at him. He'll go exactly above my head and then he'll p-parachute himself into my wool helmet in search of his ultimate Truth. And... you... Huh, you are pretty much in his p-po-SITION. Desperately trying to ascend into the land of Jazz and..." He shrugs and pulls from his pocket a piece of dark bread. "Wanna bite... No? Good. More for me."

Slowly he bites and chews on it. His eyes shut as if to remember the taste of each bite. His hands still.

"Words are YOU." He sways his silver growth of beard back and forth, back and forth. "No need of a license to drive them... or munch on 'em..." His munching becomes louder – his face happier. "Gotta drive 'em your way." He points at the cockroach and winks at me – "ahead of spying eyes... you know." The hard piece of bread is now hugged between his chest and thighs, legs bent tightly together, sharp knees pointing under the muddy flaps of his coat. Almost hiding or hugging the last piece.

"Gotta shoot 'em forward... Words are imprescribable. Like Truth. Double-faced... Mh... mh... Yummy, yummy in my dissipated and depraved sort of uncorrupt but lax and lewd and dissolutely anti-self-indulgent tummy. Funny... funny thing is money. Whole twelve '*stotinki*' I paid in order to get a ticket to talk to myself in front of an empty screen in your amusingly entertaining company..."

"You... " I try to interfere.

"I know." He swallows the last bite. Quickly gathers the crumbs from his lap and vacuums them all.

"Words and gloves – gloves and words... So much in common that it's even embarrassing to mention it. If Willie the Bard has gotten this trivial, big time reputation for being able to shake and spear the very verbal emanation of the desire to love and to be loved, it's not my fault. The color of time has been shuffled dramatically..."

"I don't think bread is good for your mind. Wanna cig?"

He nods.

We light.

He doesn't inhale it, he sucks and drinks it. Thirstily. The glow of his cig beats mine by far. Sudden lassitude has laid a hold upon his heavy eyelids. Swiftly exhales without even opening his mouth. His face looks as if it has been converted to a smoke-shooting shaft drained into nicotine-prolonged immobility.

"Words age differently. Exactly like p-people. Some are permanently flat. You know..."

He scratches his neck bandage.

"To exoticize a word order, definitely *p-puts* a strict border on different levels and labels. Ain't that clear..." His uncensored laughter mixed with smoke sounds like a heavy shower of hail against a military helmet floating through bursts of unconnected truths.

"Do you think the fucking bicyclist will ever show up?" He catches me off guard.

"What bicyclist?"

"The one with the film r-r-reels. I hope he's got a flat tire."

"I wish he was already here. What's the time?"

"How the fuck would I know. Do I look like a time defender? Sh-sh... Watch this..."

"What..."

"Don't move. We've got a friend, right here at my feet. See, nothing goes to waste. Not even a tiny, singular crumb. Only bipeds waste. But what a waste they are... Living longer than they could really have imagined back in their shitful youth. However... Watch... The unstylish anatomy of hunger I call it. The consistent but unpredictable change of power is driving the evolutionary struggle. Constantly."

The cockroach is circling the despicable island of his swollen foot. In spite of the dim light, every element of the original insect can be observed.

"Bread attracts cockroaches the way foreign lands attract military boots." My talkative companion has considerably lowered his voice but after this latest conclusion throws his head left, right and back – like a bemused rooster startled by his own salutary crowing – just to make sure there are no other bipedal heads in the theatre.

"You should look first and then say things like THAT." Finally, I have the pleasure of returning the favor.

"I know... I know... Fuck 'em. Fuck 'em."

"But what about me? Aren't you concerned that I might..."

"Fuck no. I know everything I need to know about YOU. You're so obvious you should worry about yourself. Sh-h-h... Look at the fucker. He froze, knows we're talking. Isn't it something...Decision time. He's got to decide if it's worth the risk. Reasserting his right to exist." The speaker's voice descends to a grumbled whisper and he throws me a quick, darkly energetic glance.

Leaning slightly forward, he pushes up the soft visor of his moth-eaten hat. The hungry insect casts a tight shadow on the floor, an inch from the man's deformed big toe. It appears to have already fed from its own shadow.

"All that matters right now is the phonic ambiguity of the word 'squish,'" the man says and firmly stomps his left foot onto the cockroach's glossy black trunk. Then once more he grinds it into the squeaking old floor.

"Isn't premeditated self-distraction a nice, clever, honorable way to speed up and redirect life's deadly scenario?" He drops what's left from his cigarette butt and steps on it with his other foot.

"That's what I call a common tap dance in tribute to life's symphony of separations." He carefully unpeels the remains of the unfortunate cockroach from his foot (a couple of limbs still tremble in vain)... pinches the end of the insect's abdomen between his thick, rough fingers and presses... A slimy cream-colored thread emerges.

"See... this was the roach's rectum, kidneys – intestines. A graphic visual demonstration for an obdurate, non-controversial rehearsal, unapologetically deadly and nutritious." He tosses it into his mouth.

"Mmmm – m – m... Dessert time... In the grip of my footsteps and only there can I find some farfetched substitute for black caviar. Well..." he masticates dreamily, eyes shut..." – texture and taste are relative categories indeed."

The man spits the hard shell out to his right in the aisle, then swallows. His thumbnail picks between his teeth. I witness this

8

quick hygienic procedure with unconcealed admiration. Though to look is also to be looked at.

He gives me a long stare. "Whoo boy... this special high-calorie diet–candy of royal jelly will keep me going throughout the fucking movie. You know... maybe you don't...But those things got the toughest immune system on the block. Sac-brood viruses, fungi, bacteria -- no way. Their immune system is pathetically uncollapsible." He lowers his voice again. "Pretty much like the fucking system we live in. For how many years..."

For a moment his eyes seem shut, overwhelmed by the bushy hedges of his asymmetrical eyebrows.

"Walls are built to keep people away from other people... but some walls could be demolished for the same reason. Depending on the season..." His eyes, now wide open, jump at the blank screen, the way flies pound themselves against dead flesh.

"Do you have any clue what the title of the film is? The film we'll probably never see..."

"'Nice to Meet You, My Name is Comrade Baluev.'"

"You've got to be kidding."

"No-PEE."

"Sounds promising."

"Absolutely. That's why there's just the two of us."

"So... why are YOU here?" His voice broods like a muted French horn with no keys.

"I thought you knew everything."

"I know only what I really want to know. Why are you here?"

"Because I'm not THERE." I offer him another cig.

"Thanks."

We light up. He inhales so deeply half of his cig turns instantly to ashes.

"You're hiding. That's why you're here. You stink of jazz. You better hide... "

"No-PEE. I'm not hiding. I'm here because... of a bet."

"Go on."

"If I'm able to see the entire crap of a picture I win. If I leave before the end – I lose."

"Tough... but you look like a masochist. You might enjoy it."

"What about you..." I give him a stupid stare.

"Why here..."

His facial hair bristles.

"Because there is no THERE. No matter where you go, one is always here. And besides... it was about time to meet."

Unexpectedly, he jumps out of his seat, takes his hat off and, smiling sheepishly, introduces himself.

"Nice to meet you, I am... Main Character Kaputev. Don't get up please. I know who you are. Bogoman... right?" He winks at me. "Ye-e-e-es, yes... The author is usually remembered for his main character. The character is remembered for his fucking fucked-up characteristics."

10

"What are you talking about?" I certainly feel the waxing of already risen annoyance. "You look like someone I really don't know."

"Hello... exactly. What did you expect? The view of YOU wrapped in YOU?"

"You're wrong, Kaputman. I'm just a painter."

"Just a p-p-pain-TER." He mocks my slow delivery. "P-p-pain-TERS... vainters. Empty venter. No polenta. Brooding color renter. Canvas-space inventor striving for the long-gone warm placenta. Restless fucked-up red-eyed alter ego p-p-PAIN-presenter. Oof... The only sensible thing you can do is to frame me – through your pencil – before time frames YOU."

He sighs. Shakes his disheveled head. Now his features give the impression of growing fatigue.

"I can remember my name, but I've lost my identity." His voice sounds like a suffocating surface of unremitting territorial defeats. "I remember everything colorless but... I've forgotten how to react to colors. I am exhausted... by the useless attempts and efforts required at any time to see through relentless propaganda into the fraudulent... meaningless reality of my own being – which in fact is based on the irrational dynamic of your petty existential needs. Terrible... All I can hear are the marching boots with rounded toes. They're everywhere."

The Kaputman starts crying. I mean with tears and all the side dishes of this popular human condition.

"Why the fuck..." I respond with aplomb.

"C-a-a-ause I... love m-my-S-SELF," he uncontrollably howls.

"Then stop fucking crying."

"W-w-w-why…"

"Rats… Don't know why. Just stop."

"I L-L-like crying. It's k-k-KIND of fun… you know."

"No, I don't."

"Y-e-e-e-es… A-a-a-ah yes… F-f-f-FUCKIN' f-f-FAT f-f-FUN."

"Then have fun – gung-ho motherfucker."
His nose is running. His face is turning an unspecified color.

"I don't want to change…" – he sniffles and whimpers.

"I don't think that's possible."

"A-a-a-ah… Everyone's changing… "

"Really… "

"They all d-d-DOOO. They change, to stay the same. D-d-d-dread-FUL. P-p-PLEASE do not change me."

"Who… What the fucking fuck are you? How would I possibly… I don't give a fucking shit about you."

"Aaa-a-ah… I knew it. I knew it would be hellacious…" The crying bastard beats on his knee with an open palm. Then, gasping for air, pauses and inhales in short, syncopating gulps. Subdivided approach for a more physically explicit dramaturgy.

"I am rolling… rolling… f-f-FALLING toward myself. Towards you… Shitty revolting. Appallingly gruesome… They will all think I'm suspiciously fictitious. P-p-PLEASE, p-p-PLEASE d-d-DOO not fictionalize me. I b-b-BEG you."

I slap him. He sobs louder. I give him a medium-cooked but solid punch in the solar plexus. The fucking M.C. caves in. Gasps for air. Silently. Finally.

Who's that... Is he a semi-monastic extrovert or a well-disguised Communistic introvert? Former informer (they are never former) or... a full-time lumpen, self-appointed tenuous reformer. Satan's asscrack or Stalin's brainwashed fully fucked-up suck. No difference... And that name, M.C.K. Is he kidding me? Kaputev...Too much. Too metaphorical. Even allegorical. How come with a name like that he's still not in jail? Sounds fishy. Even worse....Plotful. Probably a provocateur. He knows stuff about me. I'm cooked. "The land of jazz"... he said. That's it. They know everything. THEY always do. Last night... Does he know... It takes one fucking phone call. For fuck's sake he is sitting next to you. An accident... right. Too many of those. Well last night – that was an accident. You wish... Accident my ass. I was drunk. Sure... Drunk but not enough to forget. Everyone had a good time...

Dark.

The power went off.

"The power is off," Kaputev snivels.

"How unusual. Stop blubbering," I scold him cautiously.

"Give me a cig," he grunts.

We light.

He shifts. His elbow back next to mine. M.C. delivers a terrible, flame-saturated, pre-historic cough from the bottom of his wheezing lungs. It shakes the entire row. By the glow of his cig I can tell it's still in his mouth. Impressive. He is a pro.

"For the philistine shithead, jazz is shit. For the creative mind, even shit can be approached from a jazzed-up angle." M.C. clears his throat, then continues, "I told you already, you stink like jazz, but after you hit me you deserve a slightly bigger view of the truth. There is a positive scent, a stink coming out of you." He gives a short disparaging giggle and instantly adds – "not that I mind but you should know... It's not just jazz. It's free jazz. That's a no-no... You know... Just for your protection. Easy... Don't bristle. The beast that is man has no meaning. The goal of man..." M.C. expectorates a heavy secretion and soundly spits it on the aisle to his right. "...Excuse me... The goal of man is to be his own enemy. Cruel. Bloody. Predatory. Sheep on roads of no return. Destination – down. Underground. The clock of doom or ruin or whatever... is ticking in his chest... Your chest too, buddy. Tick-tock, tick-tock. Can't you hear it? The constant revolution of untamable fear." Kaputev dabs the glowing butt straight up in the air. Sparkles fly in the dark. "Nice... isn't it?" Then he starts humming; probably a self-invented couplet.

"It's s-s-sooo clear, o-oh m-MA DEAR... the whole idea is based on f-f-f-fucking basic f-f-fear... "

"Somebody must have thrown up on you. Or maybe... " He offers a profound conclusion.

"Shut up. The asphyxiating odor of your voice is like slime that drips from the marble slabs in a damp morgue." I give him a green light and more material for his expanding talkativeness.

"Now you're talking. Some words come from starless heavens – others from moonful hell. Thus man remains sentenced to an unbreakable solitude in the short journey across the ever-expanding and forever-contracting lies called truths. Don't be stingy with your main character. Gimme a cig."

I offer him one.

The light of the match casts its light upon his dream-filled eyes. His forehead then shoots down in a motion of certitude. His rough fingers embrace the short-lived flame of my match.

"Men... including the upper branches of their shadows – by the way, p-p-p-pun-CHING your own character won't do you any good – certainly are perpetual criminals against their own, fucked-up race. Motley gang of beauty killers. Never satisfied. Scavengers of greed and glut. Increasingly confused, abused and traumatized by the complex interpretations of their own inventions." He coughs and shuffles his bare feet. "Damn dark and nippy... ah... not bad... way better than outside. What's wrong with you?"

His sudden question startles me. Doesn't wait for an answer. "Major hangovers could be very productive. Certainly only for the creative mind. Listen..." M.C. turns his unspoiled breath towards me.

"I hate to lecture but...you really need a verbal spanking. Too paranoid ah... It's OK, I understand, but...if you don't trust your own character, who will you trust? You think I'm one of them. I'm not. Relax...huh, that's fucking funny that I have to say that."

Kaputev pauses and takes the deepest puff in the history of smoking.

"There are no covert attitudes" – he exhales. "We are a multifarious gang of consciously and unconsciously biased gawkers. Self-possessed recidivists of raging irrationality. The Politburo funnel of politics points down. Upon the social tunnels clogged by the fucked-up mind of two antagonistic fractions. Communist Party pigs and crossed-outs. Carnivorous and involuntary vegetarian chompers with a similar survival rate. Users and losers. Never winners. Most of them – boozers. Stumbling on both sides of the moat, hopelessly drowning in the boglike stage of grotesque ideological performances. Lumpen proletarian-vaudeville of subordinated bipedal realities gone rancid."

"What else?" I ask.

He shakes his head. "Tell me what happened or what didn't happen." Kaputev pulls something out of his coat pocket and sucks on it.

"How come you would like to know? You are supposed to know these things, comrade character," I shoot back.

"Listen...I absolutely don't give a fuck about your story. All stories have been told ages ago. Though I am a bit curious about how you're going to tell it and if a startled, drunk fly will come buzzing out of your mouth."

"It's too dark. You won't be able to see it."

"Young man. Tomorrow you'll be an old man. So fucking old that even the sequoias will get sick of your state of being. Maybe not... being so fucking blinded by youth and hatred of the Communist fuckers – raw, vain and self-centered son of an orthopedic surgeon – most likely you'll never make it that far. Huh... the very non-still life of life is like tennis and tennis, my man, is all pretty much about adversity management and problem solving. For better or worse, I... am a substantial part of you. You are running uphill. I am sliding down. Don't frown." His words resound ominously.

I can feel his silently searching stare fixed on my face with deep intensity. The darkness in the theatre is weakly diluted by a feeble stream of light squirting though the half-open door at the back of the room. Drafts of colder air fish at my neck with restrained unpredictability. Must be sunset time outside...

"It's not. It never is... don't fool yourself." His voice stands firm, all-embracing as if to subsume the entire anti-logic of this frozen moment.

"You call that a sunset? Sunset my prick. Even the overcast sky cannot camouflage its artificiality. Grandiosely banal. Precisely programmed and redirected. It celebrates 33 years from its first appearance. Exactly. With screaming stateliness it agitates the fraudulent successes of the shitty system carried on the exhausted shoulders of the super-dick-tated p-p-pro-LETARIAT herd. What do you know? Not much." He spits. Probably at the same spot. It's his spot.

"The bogus repetitiveness and strictly uniform sunsets, time after time, give me a permanent nausea plus unambiguous convulsions for fruitless vomiting. For the past 25 years you've been living in the same place. Isn't that so? Ever since you were born. And right there... between the dark blue walls you were partially protected from the deadly punch of the Communist virus. But even there, in the face of those restaged 9,100 sunsets you had to put up with the direct, oppressively blinding propaganda of appalling symbols cast in the middle of the burning red disk of the indifferent sun. Huh... a sickle and a hammer. Sunsetting to the West. Mindless but... mindful metaphor. Certainly the dubious brain in charge of this profound operation got executed quickly. Aren't you fucking sick of the sickle?" M.C. blurts out and blurbs bluntly of a cockroach.

"Sick of the sickle... ah," I encourage him.

"It's a cycle," he sputters.

"Hackneyed with the hammer..." I persist.

"Haggard is a better word." He must be smiling in a disturbing way. "The first twenty years are hairy. Things get habituated... then things become more handicapped."

17

"You mean heartbreakingly harnessed…"

"If not hellish." Kaputev concludes and makes a noise like laughter. "Can't you trim this fucking red beard of yours?" He shakes his head. "I know… it's a reaction. The black sweater. The heavy drinking… What a waste of time and energy. Uniform… behavior formed after images that don't belong to THAT r-r-reali-TY. Where is the fucking you of YOU? Don't you ever forget. That's me. Take a really good look at me. That's where you're going – maybe… but only if you pass the test and survive… ridiculous. But why should that bother me? Embracing. Selection is driving the process. It's all about signals. It's laughable. You think of yourself as an individual rather than as a shitty unit of a group. Pathetic. Your left profile looks like a cross between a fucking bearded cigar-chomping self-appointed revolutionary in a mossy uniform and his bloodthirsty, bereted buddy – devoted infant rapist and women mutilator… while your right profile has got a striking resemblance to the young Tsar Nicolai plotting the informal arrangements of his own execution. Impressively enough, one can detect a bubbling Ivan Denisovich-type of exuberant optimism oozing out like a noticeable lyrical gift from your brooding expression. Major depression… it's all I can see."

M.C. takes the chicken bone out of his mouth and jams it into his hairy ear.

"You stink of shit." I exhale the undeniable truth.

"You cannot think what you cannot think; so what you cannot think you cannot say either."

"With or without your rotten solipsisms, you stink like shit," I insist.

"Really... you stink of free jazz and I stink of shit. How proper actually. Harmonious, isn't it? The world and life are one." Kaputev examines the end of his chicken bone.

"I am my world." I bite on a fresh cig but don't light up.

"Certainly you are not. You are the world of your character – nothing else. Period. You are ME." He licks the yellowish discharge off the bone and chuckles. "The stench of the world is also its limit. Do not forget."

The power is back on.

A garbled rainbow of undefined sounds can be heard through the half-open door back there.

An uncannily mobile but muffled voice seems to stretch itself within diverting possibilities.

Could it be the bicyclist with the reels has already made it?

The power goes off.

Again...

One can amuse oneself with those moving shadows...

Back and forth...

Forth and back...

The wing of the squeaky door confronts the indelible silence.

My neighbor must already be snoozing.

Good. (That's good.)

Sometimes dark shadows conceal all manner of perilous thoughts

Nothing to do...

Nothing to see...

Not much to hear...

The immobility of the moment isn't unenjoyable at all.

This empty screen and that long reverberating scream last night... A memorable one. Spilled by a dismantled, drowning mind.

Thursday... the most fertile day. Doubtlessly. Was it... positively. Today is Friday. When am I going to hear such a full-throated and mournful wolf-howl... don't know if I liked it. This call of the wild juxtaposed to us – the so well tamed. Framed... planed and blamed for the rosy future of that ancient meridian. So much mud, snow and shit. Raw, moist, melting snow...

Most of the sheep were sleeping. The party was going full blast...

Anamnesis is a must for the hungover mind. A necessary procedure pushing the expanding boundaries of the suffering brain. Anamorphically speaking...

The recalling of things past plays the tricky role of an anamorphoscope. The truth behind this statement pushes vigorously on another shameful truth, possessively pulsating inside my brain-sty and dramatically affecting some inevitable but anandrous conclusions.

Each new line has got the aftertaste of well-unbalanced heavy wine.

She...

20

The sheep.

Sacrificial irreverence.

Salubrious salutation.

Sapient sarcastic sauciness.

Stop it.

Don't stop it. Keep on... Be-bop it. M.C. Kaputev yawns in my ear and tries (I can't believe it), to put his sleepy head on my shoulder. I push him away. He mutters something and leans the other way.

She and her suede coat. There... with her mother and all the others. What a bunch. I knew it... it wasn't going to be just a lunch.

One of those places. Where the smell indicates the ideological convictions of the inhabitants. It's always like this. Stale smell of garlic and fried lard. A resort of a sort... fat, square heads entertain there and get to entertain a fatter, squarer head. How come I was there... with THOSE... Shit happens.

The power is back on. Then the lights go dimmer. Is it possible... believe it or not we will actually see this shit.

Lights go dark.

The political journal is on. In black and white, indeed. As always. I like that. It's kind of relaxing... In the land of 'free jazz,' they call it 'previews.' I've never seen those but some say the previews are always in color. Must be tiresome. The previews are (the same ones say) a beforehand look at other movies. How unusual... don't know if I should trust THOSE who have seen 'previews.' They are the privileged ones.

"The World and Us'... an alarming title.

The planet earth rotates around its axis. All the continents are well defined in grey texture. The background is a grayer ocean. Properly the globe is tilted by three degrees. It rotates from left to right. On a black background. There are a couple of blinking dots which indicate that the earth isn't completely lost in space...

And... the music...

This majestically-militarian... anti-imperialistic but highly pro-internationalistic, boisterous marching music... deafening forte... thundering ostentatiousness... Stentorian accompaniment to the capital-letter-made, snake-like sign going in the opposite direction – from right to left – "The World and Us"...

Going round and round and round... the entire screen bursting with it... tumultuous march going loud and louder... and fucking louder and... and what the fucking rounded fuck is going on... and on.

Head-splitting vertigo...

My vision shouts, demands for square shapes.

Vigorously...

I feel like puking...

Then a blinding brightness takes over the entire screen. A shrilling sound of some explosion like heavy-duty kitchenware (possibly a high-pressured pot full of beans) is amplified vociferously through the big speaker under the screen. Categorical smell of burning film. The screen goes dark.

audience with nuclear outward-flowing radiation, reconfirming the unshakeable cosmic-proletarian order.

An operatically romantic close-up (from a different angle), of a time-punished, freshly shaved, dentured vulva sucking on an uncombed and alert cigar-chomping beaver, wraps up the entire glorious scene.

I hope the saliva molecules of our balder and ever-smiling cretin get intermingled and generously infused with a highly contagious splash of severe herpes. Though I suspect that this particular creature has a lot of the antibody known as "secretory immunoglobulin A." Sons of fucking Communist bitches – they both must have enchanted immune systems. That's why they belong to the same heinous party. They will live forever. Rumbunctious reaction from the aroused crowd.

I won't construct an erection.

...heroic soldiers, smiling peasants and glowing factory workers I will be forced to paint for the rest of my life. Flower-waving idiots in red tractors... "Hong, guang, liang" – bright, red, shining shit.

No matter how things change in order to stay the same, Thursdays remain more angular, more unpredictable than the rest of the days. Usually angularity tends to flirt with clarity. It seems that everyone who has crossed my life trail has done it through various passages and corridors but always accessing it through the same door... locked and inaccessible on the way out.

A steamy bowl of tripe. Crushed hot red peppers in it. The ultimate cure for an annihilating hangover. A whippersnapper with a freshly rubbed, well-motivated and succulent pussy will reseal and heal the inflatable theatre, rapidly expanding inside my head. Will cool down the meat of my anxieties.

Can't deny... The grotesque imagery from the screen, raining all over my bruised senses, has a certain hypnotic pinch.

Marvelously sweaty, king-size female welder with an oxy-acetylene torch, waving at me from the scorching hellshead inside the metallurgical smelter. Her brute masculinity is closely surrounded by metalliferously menacing looking, highly metabolic male metal workers with half metallurgical and half meteorological expressions, unfailingly grinning at one another. The one next to the metallurgical queen leans his massive scorch-proof frame upon her. He has got the intense look of someone who's passing kidney stones while being interrogated by KGB agents. Front tooth missing. Background music is Tchaikovsky's *Symphony No. 1* for piano and orchestra. The only one he wrote for piano – probably anticipating the universal possibilities for the use of this piece.

I've got this feeling, so pitch-perfect as to be nearly undetectable...

"Hey, bro -- I wouldn't say no to a cig," M.C. urges and tries to catch my eye.

"I thought you were asleep."

"Nay – y – y... those flashing atrocities up there." He bows his head. "The fluky terror which rules our proletarian situation... one feels compelled to help those who want desperately to get away from this sur-Communistic heaven." Something special is brewing on his face.

I pass him a cig.

An infinite line of tractors is plowing a muddy field on the screen.

There are no adulterous couples copulating in a standing position – alfresco.

I've got this itchy feeling...

"Confusion arises from misguided attempts to translate the laws of fear from thoughts to human language." Kaputev muses and coughs.

It was her idea. To bring her mom along. I couldn't say no. What was I thinking? I've known her for almost two years. She is the best friend of my girlfriend. And... my girlfriend wasn't even invited. In a way, that's better. Can you imagine...

"Definitely. You've done worse things." M.C. echoes and blows some smoke against the screen.

O.K... then. This fucker really can read my mind. I can't think of anything more abominable. That's it... I'm cooked. I must get rid of him.

"Easy bro... once born, one is cooked. You can't get rid of YOUR character. In order to do that, you've got to get rid of YOURSELF. Sometimes admitting the legacies of trivial discoveries will clear up the laws of some oppressing confusions. Keep it simple. Speak out. Even the laws of quantum mechanics are clear and unambiguous when expressed in mathematical equations. What's up..."

His sunken cheeks and feverish eyes leap away from me. He growls and bows his forehead threateningly in the direction of the flickering images in front of us.

"The size of her left breast..." I jerk back my thoughts with a fitting indictment and mutter, abstractedly addressing the remark not so much to him as to some invisible presence. "... Just a bit smaller than the other one, is the real reason for the persistent attraction I've been confessing upon her corseted sexuality. The texture of her mahogany colored suede coat...and the way she always leaves the bottom button undone. She's got this ability to pick me up with her chestnut eyes – the whole of me and to toss me over backward...the way a young mare throws her mane..."

"Look, look...someone is fucking riding a bull. NO, it can't be true...holy freaking fuck... see the mud and... the land of jazz, man...He's getting gored... Fantastic... What's that?" Kaputev's instantaneous enthusiasm is instantly extinguished by the following image of a bespectacled child prodigy, a constipated-looking boy, playing the violin with fierce forcefulness and determination in front of the mesmerized audience in the Bolshoi Theatre.

Then a different image quickly replaces the one of the performing genius. Big trucks. Cisterns. Some smiling men unscrew the big containers. The speaker's voice says they are angry farmers. To me they look more like cool, stimulated cowboys. Uplifted and jubilant. Milk flows from everywhere. A white, creamy river floods the entire boulevard. A group of elated children (well-dressed) are running next to the extraordinary river of milk. The speaker's voice broods about some kind of a crisis. Prices... etcetera... The thing I see is sheer abundance and happy faces. Blissfulness. It depresses me.

"See... what I mean..." Kaputev chuckles in his fist. "You should be THERE – not HERE." His eyes blazing.

"Go on, unload."

"Her coat... her boots... the miniskirts she wears. Her stockings and underwear. All that smells nice. Like the West – the rotten West. She gets it from the West. She is not a crossed-out.

You're not very allegorical, but at least now you are categorical. Don't know what happened last night but you look chewed up."

I shouldn't have gone... but I did. I shouldn't have invited her. But I did. We were eight. Five men and three women. Not a

28

good proportion. Plenty of liver lotion. The place... couldn't have been more typical. Of course, it was Ratto Stinko's idea. A hunting resort for fat-faced, thick-necked, supremely well fed and dysfunctional, highly regarded and certainly immortal party functionaries. To get out of the city and talk about the screenplay with the writer who lives not far from there. Right... a writer my ass. A fast cash biter. He calls himself a poet. Complete imbecile. The plan is to rework his latest book (insipid rubbish) and adjust it for the screen. We could shave, reshape and change everything, but the final product will go under his name. Only this way will we be allowed to make the fucking film. So that's the catch. Ratto Stinko will be the director. Myself, I – the art director in charge of choosing shooting grounds, faces, interior and exterior design, ideas of any kind...The important thing is the shitty writer (a party member of course) will get his money for our screenplay. That's the condition. However... over the past month, we have already done the necessary bending of the text. Surely his crippled book won't have anything to do with our screenplay.

"Our... huh... a collective pronoun. Our script... it sounds like – 'our dick.' There is not such a thing. 'Our dick'...WE will put you on OUR dick. No...WE actually will predispose you on, with, OUR dick. We will amuse YOU. Confuse YOU... and finally totally abuse YOU and your fucked-up expectations of what you really want. My man... a script is like a dick. A good script is like a hard dick. It can only belong to one fucking mother-sucking mind. There is no 'WE.' It is always ME. I – ME – MINE... I wish there was some wine." He yawns dolefully.

He is certainly right. But... he doesn't care that Ratto Stinko's father is a big time stinking Communist. A limper with unlimping stinky ideas. His orthodox belief in Communism plus his lifelong faithful service in the name of the bloody doctrine has assured a safe and cloudless future for the career of his son as a film director. The refusal of Stinko's father to accept the naked truth about the dogma, which has totally replaced the doctrine, has been a comfortable leverage for the messy haired, "rebellious" son.   Stinko's humble and well-controlled disagreement with the straightforward beliefs of his shambling father, plus the countless connections on every possible level inside the demagogue cloaca – based on the father's credentials – have turned reality for the young film director into a never-drying udder, hanging openly and presenting itself for complete milking.

"Almost like Hollywood, isn't it?" Kaputev whistles at the screen where a bundle of bloated smiles behind locked windows wrapped in their meaninglessness follow the grey flight of a soiled flock of pigeons. The previews are over.

Lights on. Maybe in a minute the main feature will begin. But only if the bicyclist with the reels has arrived. We don't know. Perhaps I should say, "I don't know."

"So..." M.C. inquires with a contemptuous indifference. "Your words advance with so much of the limp manner of someone embittered by the universe's refusal to recognize his true merits that probably the fermenting brine of your secretly blooming disappointments will appoint you – before the end of the film – to some infernally awkward psychotic spiral which inevitably will push you to climb the steep, sloping, tarred roof of the unforgiving hangover and yes...jump through the brewing exit of your dust-coated mental armor into... huh... the utopian domain of the very quadropartition social strive for the worldly, the domestic, the wild and the unknown. What the hell happened last night? Did you trample down the onion bed..."

"Totally. There we were. Around the table, of course. Sucking on rakija and red wine. Chomping on boar chops. The good stuff. Fireplace loaded. Full blast. Pouring outside. Cats and dogs. Inside – big room, huge stove, two kerosene lamps and the warm glow of a couple of fat candles. No power. That's the hunter's cabin – something like 700 meters above the main lodge (the fancy one) down there where the massive parties take place. Massive drinks. Massive food. Massive talk. Massive people. Massive smoke. Massive shit, indeed..."

"Wow... sounds massive. In the den of massiveness... I bet the females were on the massive side too."

"Two of them were pretty massive. Especially the wife of the anti-writer. I mean a massive jack rabbit posture with a semi-woman's face, as unattractive as her restless piece of tongue was reactive. Every time she channeled an abundant verbal puke upon me I couldn't help but envision her diaper-pale snout like a bloated corpse released from the bottom of a well, grinning toward the full moon. I was seated between my girlfriend... I mean the girlfriend of my girlfriend (who wasn't there) and her mother who isn't an unmassive woman either. But somehow still a different type of massiveness. I even would say, I think...a kind of appealing one. You know..."

"I do. Hey what's that?"

"No way. It's starting, man."

"The fucking shit is on. Amen." M.C. gives me a joyous hook in the ribs.

A desolate landscape up there.

A scape with no escape.

For no escape.

A cape.

Grey

Incompatible.

Infinite flatness.

Untrashed mended crack.

Uncanonical completeness.

Compendious mooniness.

"Wrap it up man. One word..." M.C. elbows me. "What is it?"

"Sad."

"Fuck no. Don't be melodramatic. Sad is my stomach. That's repetitious. What about the rounded floozy?"

"Depressed as a worn-out dress. But well-dressed. She and her daughter can travel abroad. Undoubtedly that put the fat wife on the defensive in spite of the fact that she and her case can travel too. On top of that, our driver, needless to say the official informer, seated on the other side of my friend's mother instantly started flirting with her and was severely mesmerized by the size and shape of her bountiful hooters..."

"Hooters...hotters...big fat magnanimous and milky suitors, roundful fruiters, hard-nosed nipple-scooters...a-a-ah...how 'bout that...he nods at the screen. Look...that used to be a woman and she's talking to women-like creatures. Kind of scary. Tell me more...you said there were three sets of tittonies around the table. What about the daughter, did she match up to the mother's dimensions?"

Now... this fucker instantly cheered up after I said the hooting word. If he is what he says he is, then what does that make me? Didn't he say that if I can't be honest with HIM I can't be honest with myself? Well... I still can't believe that he... HE... is my main character. And that "main" thing really bothers me. It's like, "Hello, I am the main one. Don't worry; your personality is not that important. There are so many 'unman' features to your fucked-up character that they are not even worth mentioning. I am the main picture and you are just another stewed to the gills painter... You know what I mean. Spill the beans." But surely I've got the choice to...

"Surely not," M.C. Kaputev hisses in my ear. "Your only choice is to remain choiceless. Stuck in this spying town. Like suck eggs – frowny clown, all dressed and majorly depressed in a stale lies gown. Gutless, spineless, lily-livered – going down. My job is just to warn you, though I'm the only jobless one in the fucking system." His angular shadow pivots his legs and sticks his unshaven chin on the flickering light of the screen.

The screen...it seems like a muted scream. The screen... so lean, but fat immodest aberration.

This running light like runny bite...

Diluted brushstrokes of colorless landscape...

A lake... that's not.

A swamp – more likely.

So big, it floods the entire screen.

Some men and women in a room.

How funny... They all look like the ones from the previews.

Yesterdays are regrettable. Tomorrow's still hypothetical. All they have are their bodies. And meals... to keep those alive. And breasts...

I don't even have a pale breath of an alibi. A slight chance... M.C. is right. I'm cooked. Any moment to be booked.

All that for what... for a quartet of well-shaped suckies and some fucking. East German jerk off.

Well... wasn't it an accident?   There is no such thing. Interrelated and interwoven everything is... beastly dive. Eating and talking. So much organic waste.

Fortunately there are rats...

Upsetting... They all talked Russian to this German fuck. More disturbingly he mumbled back in Russian too. Broken Russian in a German mouth. Sick. Hospitable slaves. Loud ones. Proud with their submissiveness. Why have those women nourished such heavy udders?   Bacteria evolve to evade antibiotics. Parasites adapt to drugs used against them. The fire in their eggs... only fire can grasp winter. Definitely they are stronger than men. The theatre of their biological performances is collateral. Collateral securities...

The camerawork is drenched with slowness. Images do not supersede one another. The camera is a snail. It tells a tale. A tale of collective anonymity. A circuit of no importance. But that looks important enough. Heavy machinery advances at the risk of diverting attention from the shrunken images of the people assisting it. They are moving forward. The slowness of the scene emphasizes their march ahead. What if the entire scene was blurred?   Wide grain texture in sepia...Then gradually getting into focus. The smallness of the people required to play their roles of people who have no roles. Their heavy rubber boots sinking into the runny mud, halfway up to their shins. No music... no voices... no sound at all. Muted reality. Unforgiving one. Camera-narrator follows the followers... men and machines drowning in overflowing mud. The boredom of the scene becomes part of the story. Like a picture hung in a somber museum. The curl of chestnut colored hair. Darkness in the dusk. A barking bitch. No sound. Hostile bare teeth. Silence gushes from the open mouth. Defenseless flesh of bare arm. Pale shoulders... paler nape...

Sure. That would've been a different film.

But why not an oddly glowing doorway? Beyond it we see a vast, infinitely open tundra. Some rubber boots and a walking stick clunking away. Long way in front of the horizon. Who is this walking man... where does he come from? We don't know. He throws his walking stick and pulls an old-fashioned alarm clock from his heavy overcoat. He is winding it and sets the alarm for 6:15.

"Hey, I bet you an old alarm clock." M.C. turns to me. His eyes so sunken, thinking about something entirely different. "The semi-female protagonist," he nods at the screen, "is not going to discover that her chess prodigy daughter has killed her father who tried to rape her, while the older brother, an ostensibly multi-sexual nice man, seduces the party secretary of the local factory who is a screaming closeted faggot who dreams of becoming a matador, but who in fact is into black men he has never seen in real life, clearly eager to explore and ready to shift his emotional interests – replacing them with suicidal violence in the name of the party's straightforward moral doctrine." Kaputev shoves his thumb and index finger in his mouth and starts massaging his gums.

It's my turn to bet. "I bet you a brand new..." My last words are completely eradicated by the deafening sound of some enormous digging device being installed on the shore of the swamp. The screen is bursting with constructive action and shouting broad faces. I've got to wait for a quieter episode.

Haven't I waited long enough to find a crack in the wall? A tiny crevice in order to claw away from the shitty system. High and massive the fucking wall is... It has kept me for 26 years on the premises of the Communist Mecca. To sabotage the Sistema... how... through a small-time movie with a Russophile director? He's got the last word. Son of a commie... they always have the last word. Fuckers... though he is well intentioned to me. Why? He came to me like in a purgatory. To forget about the privileges to which he is entitled. To drink from my unconfessed, secretly born and feebly practiced freedom. To confess to and parasitize my imagination. Right. The way I want to sabotage their Sistema, he probably wants to sabotage my muffled, fragile freedom. Certainly there are countless ways to erase and corrupt even unsprouted freedom. Physical destruction... persecution... but one of the most efficient ways is the gift of fake freedom. Fuckers... they are all fucking Russophiles. Last night...

"What's your bet, Bogoman?" M.C. pulls something from his mouth and flicks it on the floor. It sounds like a rolling pebble. "The cogitating mouth prefers a hands-on approach. Half of my wisdom tooth gave up. I believe it's your fault." He spits sideways.

The noise from the screen has been modified into some bogus dialogue between widely gesticulating, excited bipeds so we can return to our highly entertaining exchange.

"A brand new linen needlepoint in green, red, and white. Authentic stuff. I bet you that in the next hour we will not see the intensifying, incestuous love between a brother and a sister inside an indoor swimming pool while their parents are away for the weekend. Nor will we witness how their friends – two identical blonde girls, classmates from the Catholic school (impeccable uniforms) – are getting into a heated lesbian compression, bursting with an obscene degree of meticulously striped fulfillment and pedantically scripted sexuality... while the camera zooms across the firmly curled, moisturized body of a sixteen inch 'polska kielbasa,' slowly sliding up and simultaneously penetrating the wide-open body real estates of the younger girl's well-greased asshole and freshly-shaven juicy pussy."

"You really think we don't stand a chance of seeing at least half of that?" M.C. shakes his head dolefully. "Look, I don't understand one thing. Why has the zoom always been widely disdained by cineastes?"

36

"Who cares? They are shit-heads. Real cinephiles don't go to the movies. Memories of movies one likes are usually way better than the actual thing. However... our betting didn't go very far. Apparently you don't want to separate from your alarm clock..."

"Neither do you from this... I even don't remember. Did you say a wall embroidery? Why the fuck would I need a needlepoint?" He looks at me with unfeigned confusion.

"Because it's an exceptional one. Because it summarizes, because it's compendious, because it's the utmost illustration of the miserable place we live in... just picture this: A fat, square-headed, gnomish-looking stud in a white shirt. Sleeves rolled up. Rowing, facing his sweetfart. She is on the midgety side too. For some unknown reason, her shorter right arm is raised straight up above her hydrocephalic head. Neither of their faces reveals the slightest touch of specific identity. Both staring at each other in a perspectiveless swan boat across a mountain lake. Two identical swans, symmetrically juxtaposed on both sides of the boat. The swans are smiling at the happy couple. A pine tree forest surrounds the lake on the left side. There, on the shore, are two deer. Needless to say, they are twins. The left one ruminates on the grass quietly. The other one has perked up her ears. Looks slightly alarmed. I have to warn you that both deer are deceivingly bigger than both the boat and the loveable couple put together. But please don't jump to a hurried judgment. The sewer's touch has conceptualized the entire scene with some additional motives, in order to reinforce the composition of her thematic material with unshakable balance and gripping metaphor. Far back, beside and behind the deaf doe, one can see a minuscule bear cub sticking its snout out, standing up on its hind legs next to a tree. The bear cub seems pretty perplexed and looks fearfully at the opposite shore where in between the rolling hills, four liberating Russian tanks advance towards the serene lake."

"Wow...that's deep, man..."

"Wait, it's deeper than you think. Remember, she's got this limb raised in the air. Don't forget, her asymmetrical and undeveloped body is right in the middle of the composition."

"It could be a last Nazi salute to the beloved imbecile in front of her, pledging her loyalty to her beloved party, something like a final tribute to her pro-German convictions, before being multiply raped by the coming Russian liberators..." M.C. concludes dryly.

"Nice try...but not. What is glorious and divine about aesthetics is that it is associated only with the beautiful. Essentially it deals mostly with belles lettres and the fair sex."

"You mean the unfair sex..."

"Please don't...womanly beauty is infinitely divisible."

"But you said she's something like a formless, meaty absorption of an aesthetic dread, an abrasive arrangement of appalling proportions."

"Exactly. To me, probably to you and many others, but..."

Without warning, the screen in front of us explodes in magnesium brightness. Evidently the camera's prior claim on truthfulness has vanished. It is replaced by the more truthful burning of the actual celluloid film inside the jammed projector. It's lovely...for a moment we witness an amoeba-like melting formation in sepia half-tones representing the actual annihilation of the celluloid film as it speedily spreads from the blinding frame of the percolating rectangular brightness.

The lights are on. That means the projectionist must be aware of the coming meltdown. Hopefully he isn't having coffee across the street or hooked to the ticket-woman's vaginal void, so he can fix the reel problem. Usually it takes about ten minutes, but only if the projectionist is sober enough.

M.C. Kaputev jumps from his seat and stiffly moves his imposing body frame, stomping his bare feet as if walking in one place. For the first time, I realize how tall he is. At least five inches taller than I am. His coat gives off a heavy scent of tobacco.

"Wanna see the needlepoint?" I ask.

"You have it? No way. You're shitting me."

"No, I am not. I took it from the wall of the fucking cabin last night. Here..." I pull the well-folded fabric from my jacket pocket and lay it on his empty seat.

"Phenomenal..." His voice reverberates deep inside his coat.

"Excruciating, I would say."

M.C. leans over and examines the piece with aroused curiosity.

"It's a burst. A buoyant bungle of a botching burst, man. Stout burst of a massive statement. An eye fucking bender... the beefy replicas of the flatulent forms suggest a bulky sense of persisting vacancy. A clean-sweep anti-ethereal attack on the vortex of modern life. A hefty and subconscious contempt against the universal dynamism of the Futurist solution. The cheerful Nazi salute of the gnomish cunt carries the heavy load of required ambivalence, represented as a successive result of her pubescent philistinism, rendered and diminished by her sparkling excitement, suddenly ignited by the offensive advance of the patronizingly titillating shapes of the upcoming, unaccountably competent-looking tanks... driven by the tragically high-octane, super-hornifulness of canned and doomed dicks. I can assure you that the patriotic and the military theme perfectly secures the picture's profound loutish tantrum tantamount to the primitive drive, the desire and readiness of the central figure to get raped in front of her salivating admirer by the crack-brained conquerors." M.C. goggles at me and then back at the needlepoint. "Certainly you must be aware that the *'urinal guy'* was destined to reconcile art and the people. But the 'people' were not ready for reconciliation, are not nearly ready yet, will never be."

"Please don't *'people'* me. *People* doesn't agree with a hangover."

A penetrating look from Kaputev. Eyes widening. "The emancipation of stupidity is a world-wide order. No one is insured against it." He emphasizes *'it'* unblinkingly. "Can't you see that there is an obvious link between that piece of crap and the crapful speculations of some renowned Thinkers who..."

"You mean shit-heads who sobbed over the tragedy of the human condition while stuffing themselves with cheese and wine, masturbating their leftist tongues under the soulful cries of Russian violins on the left bank of Seine, throwing bread at one another and puking away existential vomit at night and lecturing at the Sorbonne in the morning. Anyway... the soprano sax is way more mysterious than the tenor," I counter.

"The soprano sex is way more mysterious than the tenor," M.C. repeats venomously. He clutches his face and adds: "Speciation occurs most often through competition in open spaces. Wow... this needlepoint really stinks like skunk, man... and this stain in the upper left corner. What the fuck is that? Is that why you bet it?"

"Of course not. You didn't bet your alarm clock in order to get rid of it, did you?"

"No, but my alarm clock doesn't smell of skunk either. And this thing... is it shit?"

"Well, shit happens. Though it's not from me. It's from the professor's hand."

40

"The professor's hand?" M.C. looks perplexed.

"Yes," I reconfirm. "Nothing good could ever happen with a scenario like that." I fold the needlepoint carefully, making sure to avoid touching the upper left corner. "Get this... respectable music professor in the East Berlin conservatory. Fascinated by uneven Balkan rhythms. Has been studying them for a while, but has never been on the exotic premises of this country. Arrives here like a month ago. A government car is supposed to take him from the train station. Sure enough, neither the train nor the car makes it on time. Typical Balkan punctuality. The guy is waiting at the station. He's got a black leather bag and his French horn in a case. A gypsy wedding procession comes to the platform. You know the picture... total havoc – music, shouting, laughter... the groom and the bride covered with cash. Tied-up chickens. Loose dogs. A screaming flock of children. Old and young – all drunk. Dancing away. All celebrating... their misery. The professor is hypnotized by the natural skills of the clarinetist accompanied by the violin, accordion, bagpipe, and a drum. The dancing gang is magnetized by the neat look of the professor's luggage. Two opposingly charged forces merge. The stronger assimilates the weaker. The quantum connection between the two particles can persist even if they are on opposite sides of the universe. The spellbound professor has been fully encircled on the same platform by a baffling universe, beyond any control. We can't ever know the exact location and exact velocity of even a single particle. By quantum mechanics tradition, the professor's black leather bag vanishes instantaneously. His Teutonic instinct for self-preservation commands him to grab the French horn and blow the brass out of it together with the storming quintet. Now the entire gang is entranced by the strange sound and shape of his unusual instrument and foreign delivery. Shanghaied by a long, invigorating drum solo accompanied by the wicked bagpipe cries of oblique angles. The professor shocks himself by releasing strangely choreographed sprinklings of notes that signal the stages of imminent deconstruction. The German drowns in shifting harmonies and rhythms. A fourteen-year-old girl veiled in red and yellow has been pushed in front of him by her mercantile father. A practiced thief and a gang leader, she drops the professor's bag back at his feet and unleashes her gruff voice with drawled phrasing. She is hamming it up... suspicious, gifted, and vulgar – she is everything the professor is not. A tough survivor of mythic resilience, her well-shaped tits jump eloquently up and down under her transparent top. 'How odd that so mediocre a tune should engender such a new expressiveness,' the German thinks. Her phrasing is one of pure color and independent form. The German is mesmerized by her timbrel robustness mixed with clipped voice appoggiaturas and seconds and sevenths and... whatnot. Naturally, he's got no clue that she is singing 'Theodora, Have You Had Supper,' a Thracian song that asks a question as old as folk music itself – 'Are you free to go out dancing with me, and to make love...' Half-spoken and half-sung, the girl puts her shawl around his pale, wrinkled neck. The German disappears inside the singing vortex of the dancing tribe."

"See, good songs are supposed to have their own colors but... none of us was consulted when the universe was created." M.C. growls portentously. "A transaction of German-ness has taken place. If his train and the driver were on time, his orderly structured German-ness would have remained intact, but there... he fell into a different vacuum of reality where the transmutation of species and natural selection react within a very different emotional charge." Kaputev slaps his feet on the floor. "Chopped-up rhythmic syncopation plus a deliciously jumping pair of suckies could easily wipe away my own tendency to think of myself as an individual rather than as a unit of a group."

"Thank you for stating the obvious but now I'm convinced that the despicable state of your feet is seriously affecting the efficiency of your mind which badly needs an urgent brain surgery performed with a German vacuum cleaner," I say while noticing the door back there swinging freely on its hinges.

42

No...the back wall did not open like a theater curtain. Nothing sublime or enchanting. I wish... there are omens in thought... the waiting is reiterated.

Waiting is reiterated.

Words are most reiterative.

Reiteration is fucking reiterative...

M.C. is saying something. Clasping his hands together. He looks distracted and melancholy. Coughs again. His voice jabbers like splintering wood. He doesn't look like a sculpture of a warrior. Too bad he is not a figment of my imagination. He said he is my main character. What does he mean... isn't it clear? I don't care. The projectionist will probably never fix the fucking problem. Last night... every day drags its last night. Even Thursdays... last night wasn't Thursday. I know that, though I'm not sure what today is. Do I need to win this bet? Why don't I get out of here? Go where... he said I am hiding. He is right, but I don't want to admit it. Scared... that's what I am. Always have been and probably always will be. Nice.

She said she needed tea with honey for her voice. She felt it was a bit scratchy. As warm and inviting as her eyes. Not enough power though. And the range... I don't think she'll be able to make it on the big stage. Most of them grow fat. Considering her mother's size, she'll be o.k.

I can see how the tall, slightly forward-leaning frame of M.C. drifts away towards the half-open door.

Last night the conversation around the table hovered between two subjects – bears and movies. How clever bears could be. How lucky the German professor is to have made a clean getaway – though it must have been a close shave. Just a sprained ankle. Could've been way more serious. Everyone asked him multiple questions. The guy looked visibly shaken and considerably confused. Too much action in two weeks. First, the gypsy wedding. Second, a wild ride in a cargo train with the whole gang. Unknown direction. Somewhere in the Balkans. Tiny village up in the mountains. An entire week of heavy celebration. Surely no one spoke either German or Russian. In spite of the language barrier, three days later he understood that he was participating in his own wedding. Needless to say, in the following days, the excessive program of feeding, drinking, and fucking took a rapid toll on his sixty-something year-old body. Chewed up by the extravagant fecundity of the tribe's procreative lust and the turbulent flux of spices raging in his newfound and very foreign, super-charged diet combined with the insatiable hunger for existence of his very young, highly aggressive and sexually gluttonous bride... the professor's internal organs were challenged and brutally vandalized by the inhospitable environmental conditions and traditionally-reasoned consistency of opposition to indoor plumbing. A very unsubtle disturbance has also taken place in his intoxicated and stripped mind. For the first time in his very structured life, the erotic function of music alone has given him a chance to understand the delight felt at the annihilation of the individual. Concurrently, the lubricating qualities of his newly acquired wife's voice and vagina – despite the limited variations of their contents – had become an active itinerary, received as a major stimulating symbol of creative ferment and anxiety. In short, the professor had finally realized that certain problems of musical pedagogy (for instance, the Olendorf system of playing the flute) no longer can be strictly confined to the paroxysmal contrasts of the analytical production of musical chimeras; but should also be simultaneously endowed with a discourse on basic pedophiliac trades, illustrating the infinitesimal portions of specific explosions readily and metaphorically transformed into pseudo-philosophical values... inadequately acknowledged and formulated as a result of long-gathered, thick marital impossibilities, piled up with depressing, arresting redundancies in the bottom drawer of his own infantilized memories dripping on the frumpy fat image of his flatulently fussy and bustlessly fusty wife, waiting in their box-like ugly apartment in East Berlin.

"They must have better projectors over there." M.C. Kaputev is back. "I talked to the man up there. He said another ten minutes or so...'Or so,' as you well know, could be half an hour or more. Give me one *lev*."

"For the valuable info..."

"No. For something way more cheerful. I've got sixty-four *stotinki*."

"You wanna kill me, man."

"What's the main purpose of a main character anyway?"

"I know. It's cruel but it's all part of the dill pickle. Here..." I hand him the crumpled banknote. His baneful frame marches away with an unexpectedly perky swagger.

Did I mention that there is a barrel-shaped, big rusty stove in the other side aisle? About at the middle of the movie theatre? That's where the better proletariats usually sit. When I say better, don't get me wrong. There are many unmentionable layers of privileges encapsulating the hard core of the iron *Sistema*. The best *comrades* surely never set their important shoes in this type of movie theatre. They've got their own. With Persian carpets, bars, smiling sluts, etcetera...they preach equality – we perform it. They whistle – we salute 'em standing on our hind legs. They order – we bark. They bark – we die.

M.C. is back.

"That was quick."

"Better quick than sick." He pulls a bottle of Stoli from the bottomless pocket of his coat. Pats it, slaps it, and throws it in the air. Catches it with his left hand and slams it on the top of the stove. The sound is impressive. It echoes in the empty theatre as if someone has dropped a chainsaw in an empty cistern.

"Even when you're sick, you gotta – must be quick as a nervous tick. Otherwise the reader will defect from your word-full peck."

"What reader?"

"The common fucked-up breeder." He juggles the bottle in the air, then aims the metal top of it into his eye socket. Pretends it's locked there. Rotates the bottle, simulating a hard pressure on his eyeball. Then gives up. "I used to be able to do that."

"To unscrew bottle tops with your eye socket?"

"Exactly, but now I can't apply the necessary pressure. Come to the bar." He opens the bottle by the traditional method and takes a mythological swig. Then passes it to me. "Ah-ah-a-a...the medicine for the masses. The pacifying juice for the slaves." He gives an elephantine burp. "Yes... oh yeah... the pulse of vodka definitely helps me to realize the relative validity of my own convictions."

"You mean contradictions..." I add while the treacherous substance tries to collaborate with the crestfallen bundle of my pickled guts.

"There... there... he's not a writer, but he's got the murky future of a fucking biter. Gimme a cig." He pulls out a matchbox and strikes. We light. He looks for a moment at the burning match then unexpectedly licks it and extinguishes it on his tongue. "Shadows... bog-like grey and slimy meadows, made of silenced shadows. The shadow of a very much existent and persistent full-time foe – it's not an easy task to overthrow. But how can you overthrow the insisting shadow of a non-existent foe..." M.C. takes another swig.

46

"Outside... things look like they do from inside my gums. You didn't miss much. Infernal, watchful circle of suspicious stares and colic hardships. All those shadows with the brooding gestures and movements of jar-confined larva, pickled in their own brine of hidden opinions... knowing everything about anything and nothing about their nothingness."
"I bet you said hi to the ticket-bitch."

"I did. And guess what she said."

"Fuck you."

"Precisely. What happened to your East German professor, before you appropriated the *Sacred Shroud of Shit*?"

"Wanna know the whole story or just the half of it?" I give him a frozen eye x-ray.

He returns the favor with a colder flavor. "I know the first part, tell me the other one."

Now it's my turn to draw from the bottle. I take two hits. I feel how my hangover gets a little thinner, as well as my patience to put up with the bizarre statements of whoever this Kaputev-man is. In a spare moment my whole being is ablaze with understanding and some compassion towards that blowsy character, and in the next moment it's drowned in sticky anxiety.

"'*Blowsy*' character. Right. Why didn't you think '*frowzy*' or let's say '*disarranged*?' You really pop on my radar. Don't you ever belittle your Main Character. The outside insider..." He grabs the bottle and drains it with unwonted speed.

"If I tell you, you won't believe me. So, I will. Only because I don't want you to believe me. All I want is for you to shut the fuck up and listen. Do you have a choice? You think you do... Hell no. Actually none. Zippo. Null. You're so shaken within yourself that you would do a lot of weird stuff in order to forget for a while the not very orderly package walking in your leaking shoes. My assumption is that you don't assume – that you're different from those outside – those absorbed by the need to perform their required roles of hopelessly fucked-up and constantly-cheated-by-life fucking extras." He shakes his head feverishly. Pale and worn. Presses his despicable hat over the flying eyebrows. He is a nut. He will make a good portrait.

"Better make it a self-portrait. Soon you won't even have a clue about who you might have been," M.C. declares, entirely calm.

"Spill the beans," I encourage him.

"So there..." He clears his throat. Composed and resolute. "You left it where the shitty professor was disintegrating into uncertain reminisces about his flatulently fussy and bustlessly fusty wife, waiting in their – I believe you used the not-so-poetic adjective 'box-like' for their ugly apartment in East Berlin. But anyway, the authorities were not waiting at all. They didn't want to have any problems with their German *comrades*. Unthinkable. Small-time, well-greased cog of a person, a quiet loyal informant for the 'Stasi', reporting on the cultural affairs front. Lost. Where? In the Balkans. Somewhere in this tiny, heroicly shitty country where... in the fourteenth century, the fucking Sultan Bayezit – "the Thunderbolt" – assimilated us and for five fucking centuries didn't stop raping our women and chopping our heads off... where then our Russian "brothers" liberated us and freed us from worry about supreme goals and free thinking, probably as a token of appreciation for appropriating our Cyrillic alphabet centuries ago... and where also we, without further delay, for the first time in the short history of aviation used hand grenades to pepper the fucking Turks from above and then instantly had to fight on all possible fronts with our treacherous neighbors, beating them but only to be later declared losers by the fucking Great Powers (England...France...) We... who had to find a German aristocrat and pronounce him *our* king. Unable to fix the shitty state of our stinking Balkan affairs. We..." M.C.'s growling voice has now applied a firm lecturing leverage on the subject. He is cooking with gas.

"...We who screwed up in two consecutive World Wars – always on the loser's side... who then cheerfully greeted the Russian tanks and remorselessly executed 100,000 of our own countrymen under the sagacious recommendation of the thick-mustached Georgian man of steel. We... the faithful Communistic dogs, submissively whining under the heavy Soviet stick swinging over our bowed bowels – well trained to shit, denounce and exterminate ourselves with the patriotic pathos of pathetic petty slaves. We..." M.C. gathers his breath. "...we can't let this German professor get lost and disappear on the premises of our beautiful geography. No... simply unacceptable.

We, who caught the Baader-Meinhof gang in less than 24 hours.

We, who hired Mehmet Ali Agca and sent him on a nice little trip to St. Peter's Square to give the Pope a fucking lesson.

We, who re-conceptualized the umbrella industry and eliminated, in the center of London, the ineffectual denouncer of our proletarian morals.

We, who managed to rename 900,000 people – 10 percent of the country's population, the entire Turkish residue. In one night only, all the Mehmets became Mikhails.

And, most importantly, we succeeded in excavating and stealing the bones of Charlie Chaplin – asking for a handsome ransom.

We...have to find the despicable German motherfucker and put him back on track." Kaputev spits sidewise. "And THEY did, as you're well aware. Instantly they arrested his teenage wife and his bird. The gypsy girl was shoved into a special school for minor sluts. The professor was sent to the hunting resort to sober up and recuperate for a couple of days. The authorities decided to entertain the guy with a bear hunt. Yes, after all those years of intensive hunting, the number of bears has reached the unpromising number of none. Not even a limping one, or a cub for that matter. The ranger said: 'Comrades, we are entirely out of stock.' His superiors replied, 'Surely you don't want to play the bear. We've got plenty of bearskins. You better find a bear. Period. An order is an order.' The ranger is a sensible guy. Doesn't want to lose his nice job of doing nothing, and go to jail. Goes to town instead. Fortunately, a small traveling circus is visiting. Uniformed, with a shotgun on his shoulder, the taciturn ranger, with an indecipherable expression, unrepentantly nationalizes the old, sclerotic bear in the name of the Peoples Republic. Drives her up to the resort. Gives her enough sugar and chicken thighs to become her friend for life. Lets her loose not far from the cabin. The next day, he takes the professor on a dangerous grizzly hunt. He even knows a couple of German words. It's a nice day. The professor feels way better after a full night's sleep. The availability of a personal shotgun gives him a considerable ego boost. The smell of pine trees, grass and dew... the sunlight and this lurking sense of approaching danger. How exciting... He even says something in German to his cool guide. *'Guten morgen,'* the ranger replies, proving that he can converse in a foreign language. An hour passes by. The terrain gets steeper. The pine trees are replaced by pine scrub. No bear tracks. The ranger is pushing his thoughts a couple of steps ahead of the professor. 'Where the fuck is that fucking clown of a bear? What if it's already dead? A night in the open... too much candy and chicken... too old to be free... fuck. I'm cooked.' The professor is lagging behind. Already tired but his Teutonic will keeps him going. He envisions the panting beast. Mouth agape. A fence of bared teeth like daggers. The grin of death... it's getting closer. Monstrous roar... thick streak of steamy saliva splashes onto his spectacles. He can't see a damn thing. Can't find the trigger. He trips backwards. Crushing talons rip his throat wide open. Heavy, burning breath suffocates him...

'Achtung, achtung. Watch your feet, man.' The ranger gives him a hand. The professor is back on his feet. *'Danke...Danke schön.'*

50

'*Guten morgen.   Zer good man.*'   The ranger feels flawless speaking this thunderous tongue.

It's no one. No bear. The professor is almost kaput. The ranger takes him closer to the main trail. Not a big meadow. There his son, a devoted mountain biker, is supposed to bring them a real German lunch. Warm sauerkraut and sausage.

'Stay here, okay...*Zwei minutes*...okay. *Ich-back No spatziren* – okay.' The ranger goes to take a peek at the other side of the ridge. The professor takes a leak. Suddenly the ranger hears a grunt. Rushes back. Points at the trail. 'There... there...' The professor can't zip up. The ranger hisses, '*Guten morgen... achtung...* shoot... shoot!" into the sunlit trail. They see an enormous head gliding above the shrub. Crashing sound of broken branches. Thunderous grunts. The professor lets loose of his stuck dick, grabs the gun and... the fucking ton of a beast zips in front of them on a mountain bike, speeding downhill. Right paw next to her forehead in a victorious, eye-popping salute. '*Mein Gott...*' – the professor passes out."

M.C. Kaputev lifts up the empty bottle and studies the emptiness of it.

"Period..." he says.

Under the sickly yellow light in the theatre his face is washed out and pale. Even the deep wrinkles have been ironed out by the murky yellow glow. Concave and diminished behind the bottle's transparent body. His eyes, once dark and penetrating, have turned as yellow as his teeth. His pergament-like head has gotten the petrified... platformized... bottleized... expression of a man who will soon be mossilized – green with fungus. His shrunken mouth tunnels the soil of muffled words as if dripping from inside the bottle.

"The identity of a person is not merely what he or she looks like – you might think. You might even believe that past experiences and future possibilities are what shape the identity of any fucker or fuckerette you will ever encounter. Wrong. Looks and identity are sealed together. No way out. One is programmed and one can only go in. Closer and close to his unmatchable DNA pinch. Bear in mind – our most treasured values are always incompatible and incommensurable... but never dare to forget that your fucked-up and frightened brain is less different from other animals' brains than you might think." M.C. scratches his neck with a demented gaze. His eyes fixed on the empty bottle. He shudders...the floor crunches under his bare feet.

I know what's going on. It's all a well-planned fucking joke. Ratto Stinko's signature. No question, that's his style. I almost fucking bought it. This guy is a nut. No doubt. One of those professional extras who hang around at the main studio of the National Cinematographic Center. That's why the fucker looks familiar. One of those eternal characters who knows all the directors, all the actors, sound-people, costume designers, you name it. Always available. One of those "know-it-alls." For small cash he can do anything. Play a drunk, a skunk, a nasty sweaty monk from before the fucking Communist Revolution. He could be a stagehand, a janitor... a messenger. That's the guy. But wait... Could it be that... no way... Stinko has already decided that "M.C." will play our main character in the film, and now the fucker is pulling my leg. Fuck it...but we have already found the man.

It took so much boozing and traveling. I got lucky. Hungover as usual – hunting for a pussy in the heat of this dusty village forgotten by Earth. In the hollow of a tree... that's where his dressing room was. A traveling magician with features positively ripe to be shot on film. Quite a face. A cross between H. Bogart and Salvador Dali, divided by a nose which has obviously suffered stormy encounters, but has been in faithful service to its owner in hard and harder times. The outline of this memorable proboscis has definitely surpassed the physiological and suppressed its basic, functional qualities. It has three well-defined curves. One natural one and two man-made corrections.

The profile of a waterfall with no water... A ski slope in the early stage of construction.

In my opinion, he was the man we needed. Damasko – his name. Sounds apocalyptic. He appeared to be the most vivid character from the dozens of professional actors tested in the past months. After a monstrous drinking binge, Damasko made a threatening confession that, throughout all his life, he had been dreaming of playing a cowboy – the bad guy of course – in a real "spaghetti Western." I was certain that the unique nose-holder would go nuts if he got the offer to play the leading role of a painter-artist in a spaghetti-free and very un-independent film. Poor man, he will act like a failed magician with an uncertain cowboyish attitude... totally misplaced in a bogus pseudo-punk operetta, bursting with repulsive metaphysics. That'll be something. I voted for him.

"How many roundabouts can you possibly square..." M.C. jumps the train of my gallivanting thoughts.

"More than you, for sure. How many squares can you roundabout?"

"That's what I do for a living, man."

"It doesn't seem profitable."

"Habitable, of course. But more important, it's indubitable and inductive." Kaputev completes the phrase without looking at me.

"Productive..." I press.

"Deedy and deductive." He stresses.

"Constructive..."

"I would say predictably restrictive but addictively vindictive." Motionless by the stove he looks down at his feet. "I hate socks." M.C. adds with agitation.

"You don't know the pleasure of mending a pair of worn out tennis socks."

"Huh...Fiddlededee. Fictive statement. Fiddle-faddle f-f-frequen-TATION. Fuckin' fidget noun. You fuckin' made me stutter and sound like a fucked up, finny fidfad. Fuck that... we will never see the entire fucking movie. Twelve fuckin' stotinki I wasted for... your highly entertaining company. And you know what?" Now M.C. concedes gloomily, almost menacing – "I know exactly why the fucking projectionist can't fix and put together the fucking reel. Because he wants to fuck the cashier-bitch in the ass, because the sucker is so fucking romantically in love with her that he envisions her shitty butthole as a galvanized shrine of her sheer, picturesque, rural provincialism; he glorifies it as aliveness, as a primordial sort of burning epicenter, a tireless... tire-shaped, pressurized, individual shaft for expulsion of her rural nastiness and fully processed toxins... where the finitude (or the broken bio-furniture of fast-food related products) of Nature's grinding circle has been manifested with such clarity and disambiguity... where only his prick could possibly carry on a deeply respectful mission of truthful love – emission and monition." M.C. looks around the theater and repeats, "Monition..."

He pulls his alarm clock out of his pocket and studies its beaten face. Then mutters to himself, "...How much can be seen in a woman's ass if one keeps looking at it for no reason?"

The lights go off. The light on the screen grows louder and louder. Violently upright. Pitchforks and axes marching over the hill. Nameless creatures and a dog. Several goats and tractors. They all are going somewhere... They pass a wooden roof sagging in the middle. Shadows of high-tension power lines slice the clouds in even strips.

54

Parallel proposition.

More of it...

The cameraman makes his point.

Running child. Barefoot in the mud.

His mother is everywhere at once.

We don't know who she is...

She is a part of the people who aren't trying to be people.

They are trying to be parts.

She is a part of them.

Parts and their shadows.

Mouths crying out a song of togetherness.

But no sound.

There is an old man. He takes his hat off. (Wow... That's Kaputev's hat.)

Everything sounds soundless.

The strangeness of soundlessness is complete.

Properly placed...but not.
"Isn't it great? The fucking projectionist lost the sound now. Lucky we. Unexpected bonus. Free from the grasp of sound. At last..." M.C. sighs motionless by the stove.

Don't know how lucky I am. The interception of voice could be intermittently interfering. Cramping... dragging upon what... the grim stretch of post-war, laborious, Soviet delirium – muted. Concurrently, the idiotic images presented without sound – lubricant becomes slightly more sensible in their deaf poignant fate. Their fate... the outline of *my* fate right now looks positively super-bleak. Certainly I will be investigated. I'll be cooked...

"Too late for that. Your '*I*' has already become a fearful eye. I hope you've got no regrets." M.C. clears his throat and looks back at the dark doorway. The door is shut. "Plenty of drinking and fucking doesn't necessarily lead to cirrhosis or venereal disease, but the right proportion between those two activities could prevent unwanted consequences." For a moment he looks straight up at the ceiling, probably expecting another cockroach to descend. Then his stare stubbornly drills into my face. "Gimme a cig kiddo. Don't fret. You *had* to do it..."

"To do what?" I pass him a cig, but I know that he knows. He rubs his rough thumb with his fingers. The shifting light on the screen gets brighter. The shadows on his beaten face grow darker. His lips move dryly and blow smoke against the screen.

"You had to let him drown... I mean, your entire life has unfolded, has rolled upon that particular moment when you decided to release your grip and let him go. That's understandable. You're no gondolier or furniture mover. The whole unedifying mess of the evening's pitiful progression (digression if you will) was driving you exactly towards this focal point of fecal disaster. Every disaster deserves its master... you know. Look up there, the screen is ignited by a major disastrous flow of time – some call it life, others history or even a movie. They all need food and fuck... you too." M.C. draws another deep puff. "See how beautifully they are muted. I believe sound brought unbearable limitations to the talkies. However... I hope the fucker up there won't spoil the show by fixing it. See... those up there are draining a fucking swamp somewhere in fucking Siberia. Bad news for us... but worst of all – we are watching them doing it. That's a vastly convincing symptom of a multiple massive depression. But don't worry... it's all tied up with the events from last night. That is to say, the structure of reality... I mean, the vacuum."

M.C. yawns, his eyes shining. He starts humming but his voice uncontrollably derails and begins to rattle like empty carts rumbling over a rusty bridge:

> " – gonna dance my stenchy coat away
> yesterday's regrettable and tomorrow's
> hypothetical..."

An eye-bruising beam crosses the darkness and a high-riding wave of cool illumination splashes back from the silent screen at M.C.'s unkempt facial shore. He doesn't blink. Only his hairy nostrils widen as if sniffing out the newly formed image up there.

"I hate to be brief... I'd rather be a thief. Briefness is a sign of spiritual deficiency. I hope you're aware that in the land of free jazz, most of the mortals are pretty brief. They work hard. That's why their real music is hard. Remember the man with the plastic horn... he said, 'Music always brings goodness to us.' Can you imagine?"

"But that's not all he said," I interrupt. "The alto-man added, ' – *unless one has its motive for a different use.*'"

M.C. frowns. "I see, I see... the buzzing bee of your be-bopped esprit. You've done your homework, o.k. Don't perk up now. No time. I hate to be brief... I'd rather be a rotten leaf..."

"Well, a '*fallen*' would be a notch more poetic," I persist.

"Persistent and insistent but... listen to that... can't you hear it? Tick-tock, tick-tock... so close to my testicular-bursting pack. We've got the sound of tick and tock... the voice of time gets bloody like fermented wine. Time has grown into a sign of prowling lateness... four minutes left."

"Wanna shut up then..."

"I'd rather give you the verbiage. In the long run it might be useful..."

"But, don't you hate to be brief?"

He cracks a crooked, toothless attempt at a smile. "Right. I'd rather have some beef. So... a stale stench of garlic, linoleum and Marxist-Leninist ideology. Stuffed buck's head on the wall facing the big, retouched photo-portrait of the fucking father of the Nation. All of you around the table. Loaded on meat, wine, and rakija. Compressed little company of obedient, tiny souls. Soviet ass-lickers. Chronically afraid and envious of one another. Fidgeting informants, collectively aroused by steady Politburo propaganda. They all know, you're a '*dubious subject.*' But some of them know 'bout you more than you do 'bout yourself. No biggie... you're seated between the mother and the daughter. The fat wife of the pseudo-writer across the table is torturing the biggest accordion ever. But the worst of all – she is singing. Her bloated, red-cheeked face is perspiring with an impressive determination focused on the clumsy movements of her own sausage fingers, tripping over the keys. You wanna strangle her but instead you're fingering the tightly-jeaned crotch of the opera singer while sucking on the wine and thinking, "*...They share a special kind of metabolism. A world of their own. A world I'm determined to escape. Thirty fucking winters passed by and not even a chance to reach the starting line. Like a downhiller going up... like a slalomist stuck at the first gate made of bricks and bars, higher than the mountaintop, longer than the equator, solidly erected in all four directions. Not only that but... anchored on THIS side of the Wall... no fucking chance to cross it. What am I doing here with these shitheads sitting on their hands and brains?* But then you feel her mother's right hand massaging the profile of your prolific tool under the table. *Pussy-matt rat... clitor-*

58

bureaucrat...   asshole   tutor...   crossing   women's   genital geographies has been..."

"Hold on. Time's up. You crossed the four-minute benchmark, I think. Secondly, your aptitude to be brief and to the point and their abilities to drain swamps," I nod towards the screen, "obviously have some similarities."

M.C. shakes his head. "You don't know what's coming, do you? Clueless. Lucky fuck... you. An artist with no watch." He pulls his alarm clock out and shoves its greasy face into mine. "It's five minutes ahead. As always." He spins his tongue and rolls the words like a hissing, drooling valve passing spitful burping exclamations. The exodus of his freshly fallen tooth makes him more convincing. "As always, ahead of time – in my own time and never on time. Got it? I hate to be brief but someone has gotta be the reef against time's fucking referendum. Hah ... repugnantly brief – such a relief to riff and biff some bi-forked truths on the wall of life's dull and somber hall. One must maintain the utopia of suppressed dreaming." M.C. carefully displays the alarm clock on top of the stove, right in the middle of it. Then he positions it facing the screen so we can witness the imminent passage of the next several minutes.

"Twenty-four times a second. Twenty-four frames of galloping time racing the preclusive aspect of abominable present unrolling..." M.C. looks at the flickering images. "...but still, nothing happens. That's serious. I expect they don't expect to install that enormous pipe and suck the fucking swamp out. No way... that would have been a bummer. Then what? Another swamp – another pipe. More mosquitoes – but a thousand miles away. In many ways *'they'* are like you. They like to suffer on their own turf. Not that you are a major sufferer but... the world belongs to those with teeth." M.C. pauses and puts his dirty finger into the freshly formed, bloody hole inside his mouth. "Just to make sure it'll grow again." He spits. "Three pairs of tits and five dicks could spell the right proportion for an unplanned plot."

"Too much spice. Too much bratwurst. Too much excitement. They all agreed. The German was lucky. What if the bear had crashed into him instead of into the police car down there on the main street, a few blocks away from the circus? Sure enough, she didn't know, the light was red. Even if she did, the bear had generated too much speed already. Considering her weight and advanced age, there was no way she could possibly slow down and avoid the uniformed fuckers. The driver was hurt but the other policeman shot her on the spot. The bicycle – recycling item of course. The ranger and his son arrested for unpremeditated negligence. All the trouble for this German fuck who, on top of everything, got diarrhea last night. At the wrong place and the wrong time. Exactly while you were shifting gears between the pussy property of your friend's girlfriend and her mother's back burner. The visceral punch lines of your prickful altruism found a certain array of recognition among particular type of 'fe-mammals.' If forty-five minutes is the perfect amount of time to get to know the Prado, then half that time could be sufficient to get acquainted with the pelvic strategies of two blood-related cunts..." M.C. gives a rhinoceros sneeze. His face twists with melancholy pensiveness. Feverishly pulls out a very white, very silk, very ironed and impeccably clean, very neat handkerchief. One never knows what one might encounter. He covers his entire face and delivers a challenging elephantine honk. An intense oomph behind it. Do I see a nice little monogram – M.C. – under the jumpy reflection of the pale light, embroidered in the corner of the loose end?

Excessively symbolic, the panoramic landscape behind M.C.'s standing frame is juxtaposed to the hyper-active ebullience of some monotonous bonding of men, machines and masculine-looking females.

"While fucking, one can't go beyond the boundaries of structure." The soundtrack of his voice is now imbued with an overriding preoccupation with his own delivery.

Considering the circuit of circumstances, it's o.k. to have someone reciting what happened to me last night. In fact, the longer I listen, the surer I become that having any hope for control over my own life is a groundless proposition.

"No matter what, elaborating on the raw materials from the compositional content of female fluids isn't. But... in spite of the fact that you are liable to spend the rest of your shrinking life drilling and probing the conjectural roundaboutness of female flesh with no chance to understand it, that doesn't mean you shouldn't. I know the more inaccessible a hole is, the more deep research one wants to apply to it. Like going to church... anyway... you went outside with the opera singer. To get some fresh air after the rain. Under the stars. Those constant cosmic scars... cut into the effervescent pill of this eternal wheel. You felt her perky pears... you followed the assiduous itinerary of your male instincts. The eternal script of unapologetic horniness. By the way...wasn't it ignited by the mother's grip under the table? Surely it was... dusky foliage. Bright moon. Your blood closer to the skin. All drained into your genital package. The squeaking of her leather boots. The whole display of her walk. The threshold of her silence. The smell of rotten grass. The empty hour and the Prussian blue above. The wet... carnal sound of cream under her slow, dubious steps. Your hand at her waist. The wool skirt. The zipper. The pull. The yellow of your desire. The milky pink of her panties under the pine tree. Your finger – her clitoris. Her paw – your balls. Panties down, piston up. Well-groomed pussy mouth. Halting place. She grabs the tree. You shove it in. You give her a worthy pace. From behind. She yeses you with panting praise. You give her a higher octane pace. And you are thinking about 'the circle with the hole in the middle.' He named a song after it. You've got the album. You've got your usual fascination with abysmal forces in a roundabout way. You've got the playful mantra of her vaginal mischievousness, but... but while pumping her, you are thinking about her mother's ass. How she was fanning herself with her favorite proletarian newspaper. Trying in vain to compensate for the decreasing estrogen production from her ovaries. You see... look how every fucking detail fits into the entire puzzle of the shitty being. There..." M.C. nods at the screen.

Man with a hard hat... trying to unscrew a huge bolt right above his head. Four cable winches support a swinging platform. On his knees, the man tries to maintain his balance on this tiny rectangular island hanging in the middle of nowhere. The platform starts to descend. It gets closer to a big control board. Big red button. The man cracks an unhappy smile and picks up a gigantic wrench. The tool is as tall as his chin above the platform. Looks like a crutch. Everything appears to be over-sized but the people. Huge pump... it sucks the slime of the bog as if...

"... as if God's dog has just drowned at the bottom of the bog and now everyone is rushing to find the fuckin' bitch," says M.C. and begins to count on his fingers.

Men dressed in bib-waders crawling inside a metal parallelepiped shaft. On all fours. Advancing their slime-smeared poker faces directly towards the camera's still eye.

"Crossing women's genital geographies is like crossing territories of unshared expectations – essentially speaking. We are liable to spend the rest of our shitty lives fucking stuff that won't tell us what we want to know. Sure, you've got no choice. You've got to keep doing it, but that truth comes at a cost..." Now he is looking me straight in the eye. "Pussies may not be inviolable but certainly they are infinitely variable, to my humble estimation. Or at least they struggle to acquire a new identity on a monthly basis and *that* definitely messes with the marrow-mind of every new prick probing their juices. The banal windy contingencies, the trivial shibboleth that the egg-holders are the weaker sex, have made you an even more persistent beaver-cleaver – fast retriever in a *Sistema* where betrayal is the only currency. So... twenty minutes later you took full advantage of her mother's menopause onset. You took her for a short, nice midnight walk. No talk. Needless to mention, to exactly the same pine tree where you have just thoroughly rattled the daughter's hotter pussy. Same moon. Same full-blown gloom. But a different body's thermo-neutral zone, spiced up with a touch of brain norepinephrine... just enough to keep her menopausal flashes up and her brassy butt as hot as a China cup on top of a constipated gut. But then... she spat on your bratwurst before you opened her as wide as she would go and rammed your bulbous plonker in. She cried, but committed her 100 trillion cells to the pain and submitted her Communistic sizzling self like a newly discovered, partly fermented perimorph to the vigorous pumping routine of your probing spermatist. Her panting at the door of starry silence. Your surly face... her blonde, lamentable existence, obstinately projected through her uneven sweaty breath, racing at full speed. Your middle finger, now stuck between her teeth. The rustle of the leaves... your full hand milking the swinging volumes of her heavy breasts. But all that... not enough. Still... something is missing. You would have liked to finish this proto-realistic fuck in her mouth, to rinse your pleasure stick with her saliva, but... you see a flashlight. Unsteadily advancing towards you. You pull on her hair and shush her. Still your cock is only halfway in. Could that be her boyfriend? Unlikely... by now he must be urgently, unflinchingly conquered and exalted by the improbable enormity of the writer's wife's hooters. The flashlight changes direction. Hesitatingly describes a circle. Uncertainly rushes to the left and to the right. Falteringly zig-zags towards the bushes. Vanishes...you give her a rocky push. Your cock slides in deeper. She cups your chilled balls with an unadjusted sigh. Someone is screaming... but it's not her. Short, even shouts. Incomprehensible. Short, obscure, scraggy cries. Must be in German. Must be the fucking German. The indecipherable pleading comes from beyond the bush. What's wrong with this nut... is he a fruit-picker, or have his recent Balkan experiences shaken his presumptions about life and his ability to put up with it? Annoying...who needs that mess? Surely your cock does not. The gravest insanity is to interrupt a fuck. Those screwy... queer shouts... how bothersome. But you'll be damned if you'll stop humping. Gotta keep on truckin... gotta bulldoze... gotta brush it... bruise it... brunt it... gotta fuck it. In the somber beauty of the night. But... the fucking jackass won't stop howling. Unexpectedly she races away from the grip of your dick. The root of your precious penis jumps up, involuntarily freed from its tight quarters ..."

M.C. completes the last words with some frozen fish of a voice. Barely audible. Inquiringly, his eyes study the motion of somber sleuths who have gathered around a female protagonist (the latter is dressed in heavy working gear – like a man). The camera pulls back. A panoramic scene with a lot of people standing around what looks like a freshly dug grave.

"See..." he whispers. "The temptingly convenient role of the soundtrack, totally eliminated."

"Convenient for who?" I inquire.

"...Neither the noise of the crowd, nor the crowing of the cocks, nor the barking of the music and the dogs could now spoil the well-behaved mystery of the limited infinite on the fucking screen." He is nodding in approval. "But the soundtrack of unfilmed reality spoiled your fuck last night," M.C. casually observes and continues.

"Never less than excessive and too often excessively symbolic, your militant copulations are still able to amalgamate, or integrate, or merge, or... mix or even fix the unsober agencies of your eyes, hands, or fucking feelings (if any) of visions, or whatever comes along on your bleak agenda to unite with... your chronic anger."

M.C. gives me a searching look. Suddenly snaps his fingers and sings out loud in a raspy baritone, "...*anger...anger is the super banger.*" I'm convinced he's just made it up.

"So... there." M.C. burps unblinkingly, his eyes widening. "The picture isn't necessarily picturesque. While she pulls her panties up, you manage to wipe your dick on the underlining of her black leather coat. She owes you a five-fingered Merry. There is a commotion back there, around the cabin. Someone is running back and forth with a flashlight. No more shouts from the German jack-off. The man with the flashlight is the mother's boyfriend. He storms out of the cabin, but this time he's got a long rope hanging around his shoulder. He runs toward the bushes. Trips on the rope. Flat in the dirt. Gets up but you can tell he's drunk as hell. Yells something. Disappears into the bush. You follow him. The shit-house. Rotten barrack. Yes, you know the structure. Everyone who's been a soldier knows it (in this geography, anyway.) The smell – inhuman. But you are outside. A flashing thought flushes away everything else inside your head. Only humans are able to produce such an invigorating stench. The man with the rope bravely enters. You are four meters away from the door-less doorway. The army has given you a priceless lesson: If possible, keep a good distance from the shit of others.

The moon is peeking halfway through a cloud. You can see o.k. outside, but the real action usually takes place in hard places. However... you can barely see the back of the man with the rope cautiously advancing forward in the dark following the slim line of his flashlight. But then, unexpectedly, there is an instant flash of light coming from the opposite direction. A thicker stream of light stronger than the man's flashlight unexpectedly confronts him – and you. Now you can actually see the rotten floor of hell. The missing planks. The twelve shit-holes overflowing with shit and newspapers. It takes you a couple of seconds to realize, to acknowledge the source of the light streaming against you. Your brain is slow. The unimaginable supreme splendor of a hostile, proto-barbaric stink has replaced the air with the mind-fucking reek of para-infernal human waste. The light runs from the seventh hole. Biblical number... there is a piss-head over there. Covered in a hardhat with a miner's lamp on it. Almost at floor level. We all know to whom it belongs. Of course, to the fucking German professor. Color drained from his face and painted brown... eyes feverishly racing towards the light searching his horrified face. That's right. Up to his chin... strangled in a straitjacket of shit. Some things are meant to be. Though still somewhere in his smeared facial cantaloupe one can detect a grain of quickly fading hope. It's focused on the rope. By now your eyes are desperately trying to help your nose forget the fetid grip. But... your entire self has boarded the train of stench that is now running so fast towards the deepest, most unconceivable rancid authenticity. Speeding on the utmost triumph of that unbearable stench. Tangled threads of flashlight in front of the entangled, unsure steps of the drunken man in front of you. The squeaking, soft planks and long rusty nails protruding out of the entire structure vibrate like a damp, worn-out cardboard box. His soles sink into shit-soaked ramshackle, putrid wood. The adamant perfumery of Acheron is so brutal that the savior's brain is clogged by the deplorable account of organic miasma, paralyzing the very notion of smell. The condensation of excremental gas is so high that it makes even you, situated at the missing threshold, sick and ready for a major midnight puke. Well... the extraction of this sunken human tooth from the heavily fermented and pickled in piss, shit-slime-cavern can't possibly be a walk in the park. The half-assed helper makes a half-hearted throw of the rope. The rope's end lands about a meter away from the frightfully frightened and bloated head. The unfortunate professor must pull himself out of that shit and reach for the rope if he wants to continue his miserably flat life. The other guy – the driver for the government – is reluctant to make another step towards the middle of this already half-sunken shit boat. The last thing these two can think about in this very moment is... what you're thinking. The laws of any ideologies and institutions, closely corresponding to the physio- and bio-laws of shitting plus thermodynamics. While attempting to breathe through your mouth only, another conclusion is buzzing inside your dazed brain. Neither justice nor injustice could possibly juice up the already shitty situation. By now, you are more than certain – the next minute or so should be a very fertile time. But in the meantime, the professor desperately tries to simultaneously raise his left elbow and right hand above the broken floor of his bogus trap. His hand frantically paws the

66

slippery edge of the slimy plank not far from his nose, while his elbow slowly surfaces the brownish fecal matter and intensively tries to hook itself to the sickening wood. His motions look oddly cottony and hollow. Defiantly, he bursts his gut and exerts himself in a vain attempt to kick and have a shot with his legs but the gloopy nature of his new and extra-challenging environment doesn't comply with his supreme efforts. In all of his endeavors, his bald pate, in a very slow and swinging motion, pops up and down, like a tightly anchored buoy struggling to resist the rising influx of some horrendous, glutinous tide of clammy excremental marmalade, pulling him down to the bottom of this viscous, miry well. You start to wonder, what kind of a swimmer (if any...) was he in his youth and was he ever any good at the butterfly? However, the momentum is firmly working against him. His head drowns to eyebrow-level, and he is slow to recover to a breathing position. Evidently... unforced errors leak from both of his wings and legs. But one can understand that... he's got a lot to look forward to... At the same time, the other one flicks the rope in an attempt to aim it within reach of the drowning head. His attempt is far from successful. He can use only one hand. With the other, he's got to keep the flashlight aimed at the subject of his attention. The jerking and life-demanding commotions of the head conduct unpredictably tangible illuminations all over the place. Considering the special circumstances, the distance between the two active sides, the poisoned breathing conditions and the slippery conditions, you're less than optimistic about the final meager scene; mise en scene if you will... but... you see... my knowledge of your past is just an approximate memory of an approximate hypothesis." M.C. speaks fervently, while suppressing a shudder. Then he continues. "Thus, resistance to gravity is not necessarily resistance to death in some cases. The fucked-up head is able somehow to gasp for air. A paramount effort to pull itself up. Both of his hands shoot for the treacherous wood. Splitting sound... a big chunk of the floor dislodged... levered out... the split is instantly followed by a noisy splash of fecal matter raining down on the petrified professor's head. The intensity of the action makes you feel somehow excluded and firmly assigned to the place of the witness. The effect of over-determination, the tenacity of life's last push, the grotesque density of convulsion, muscles widening the jagged parameters of the shit-hole and miraculously enough, bringing the rope down into the bubbling miasma. The end of the rope is now on the top of the broken, sailing-free plank, advancing slowly upon the dispirited eyes of the agonizing musician. Then a highly wired effort plunges his hand on the rope's end... and the excessively insistent urge for survival launches and he locks his other hand to that life-promising line, reconnecting him to some instinctive, scarcely sustainable hope. The unexpectedly firm grip pulls the other guy forward. Holy Moly... the driver jerks ahead like a high-powered trolley. Clumsy footing... he stumbles and the floor gives way, splits in two with an impressive crack. His body tilts until it loses its balance, his free hand wildly paddling the air in a windmill motion. In vain... he can't regain his stability. The floor shoots out from under him once again. Loud smack on the surface of the fecal slime. Fate drives the driver into a freshly formed hole, but with a bigger diameter than the one where the professor has settled. Now we've got a really tricky situation. We have two members of the same party, drowning in the same shit of the fervent defenders of their dear regime, still connected by the same line. Metaphorically, allegorically, symbolically and historically speaking, the situation couldn't be more satisfying to your understanding of justice. It's a juicy one. Considerably darker too than a moment ago. The driver's flashlight wasn't shit-proof. The action now is lit only by the frantic commotions of the miner's lamp. The international proletariat thrown into their own brine of socialism – a fantastic utopia. The worldwide liquidation of the fucking commies – how sweet a dream that has been... but hey, now you are at the threshold of something with a positively optimistic denouement. Shit happens... it's a matter of fact – shit matters...

So... the driver's face is bleeding but the rope is still bound to his left wrist. It's a tug of war. The rope is strained to the breaking point. The distance between the two shit-holes is about four to five meters. The side that wins will live. Competition is great nutrition. Just beautiful... now, everything is fair. Ornette once said, 'If one can't find the straight line one must zig-zag unless he finds the circle.' The deadly race is properly staged. The bad morals of the competition have infected both participants. It's written on their agonizing faces. Curiously enough, you can't tell who's gonna win.

'Fine feathers make fine birds' is not a proper proverb for this particular moment.

After the fall, the new player (way younger than the other one) has apparently swallowed a generous amount of shit. Can't maintain the coherence of the flavor. Coughing... jerking... trying to swim... gasping for air... in vain. Too much effort for his drunk body. Botched job...

Meanwhile the German contender has gotten two points of relative stability – the rope and the floating plank. On top of that, he has learnt something in the past five minutes or so. Less is more... economically he uses the counterbalance on the other end of the rope and very slowly but surely advances towards the wooden shore. Even the lamp on his head is now steadily beaming forward. The suspense of the moment is subdivided in two original ways which experience speedy developments. The excremental slime climbs the proletarian profile of the driver. From your point of view, you can only scrutinize his actions and the expressions of his right profile (needless to say neither profile is photogenic considering the situation.) In a moment his play would therefore be the ultimate gag. Thick, brownish bubbles simmer around his drowning pate. Only his hand, with the rope wound around the wrist, remains above the surface. For this brief fraction of galloping time, the professor has already managed to pull himself halfway out of his hole and is now gathering his breath. Face down. Hands still clutching the rope... shit-wrecked... takes his time, but time is running out for the other contender. You can see -his fingers let go of the rope. Convulse. Tremble. Still. We've got a winner, but still he is far from safety. Very slowly – using the counterbalance of the drowned man on the other end of the rope, the German crawls and gains a balanced position at the center of his unreliable raft. What a picture represents is its sense. And definitely its space too. I call it spice... however – back to *your* story. The hard-fought one meter of territory our professor has gained going up and forward is exactly one meter of territory the driver's corpse has lost going down. The stretched hand has disappeared below the surface. But still the tension on the rope has increased considerably due to the fact that the entire stiff is now pickled and stuffed with shit. Now the survivor lets the rope go in order to free his hands and paddle to safety. Like a startled snake, the rope instantaneously shoots at least two meters down. Fucking deep – the corpse pull."

M.C. clears his throat. "One of the first principles of warfare is to seize the high ground – that is to go up (same principle applies to real estate.) Everything else becomes vastly reduced from that vantage point. Now...similarly this flatworm of a man – this 'Stasi' motherfucker informer maneuvers towards the doorway. Towards you... well, opportunities haven't knocked on your door very often. Your mind starts to race like a lemur's heart. Wanna kill that son of a bitch or let him live and continue to spy on other denouncers? What about you... how is he going to report what just happened? Are you willing to take the risk and let him live? Huh... some smells can deform a man's thinking by a no less imperative necessity. A slime lizard of a man in excremental armor. Back to firm land. Panting like a prick in putrescent shit. Nearsighted sycophantic trudge of crap. No more eyeglasses. Can he recognize you? It doesn't matter. The moon is high and full of gloom. You've got to go. But... what's this sound? A hunting hound... or fucking ball of fur... wow... so neat, it looks like a skunk. It sprays the crawling turd of human punk."

Dead silence. M.C. shuts his eyes. His expression is of a man who rests on a bench, watching the storm of a summer night. The light from the screen lurks and haunts his face, revealing the murmuring wash of murmuring merit. The two-dimensional images are swallowed by the camera's boring contrivance, capturing the swarming movement of people possessed by the frantic impulse for togetherness in the absolute brothel of labor.

Pitchforks, axes, shovels, hammers, and spades...

Tight-lipped rudimentary shapes...

Sealing the vents of proletarian proliferation...

Stenographic abbreviations of monumentally diminished bipeds in a dilapidated state of mind...

The aggregation of the ultimate aggrandization of Communistic history unrecognized as punishment for being born...

"Fuck that... the aggregation and the aggrandization of your sick dick makes you dispute that visual Soviet puke." M.C. points at his clock.

"No matter what, one is always late. Good luck..." He takes the aisle seat next to the ice-cold stove and pushes the worn-out wool of his hat down over his eyes. Crosses his hands on his chest – chin down – ready for a nap. I take the seat in front of him. My hands in the pockets of my forever jacket. The lining is colder than the outside air. There is a hole at the bottom... by old habit, my index finger feels the hole's boundaries and confirms that the opening is bigger than yesterday. So I might be able to insert my middle finger through it and make a brief assessment of the fluffy darkness and... determine the distinction between past, present and future. In vain... an illusion – in spite of the oily sunflower seeds nestling at the bottom. Holes, no matter if dry or juicy, are usually dark or even black and they provide the true frame of reference for defining motion. Why do the veins of my basic expectations envenom me and channel my efforts to find myself elsewhere... who is this person behind me? Right now, why am I in front of him? Is he annulled by reality or on the contrary... the darkness or the light are describing this luminous rectangle in front of me. The larger the image – the lazier the eye – The worlds of drawing and fucking have always been...

What's that? Someone isn't trying to avoid the loud noise of his hobnail boots stomping heavily on the squeaky floor. The joints of my shoulders become stiff. I must not turn. One after another...the heavy boots echo against the floor and the transparent silence. Isolated, superior footfall. Getting closer... getting louder... right now the fear is my time. The story is my story but... the moment unfolds with the repugnant predictability of something I've anticipated for a long time.

The inevitable happened. Warm-up is over. Now all depends on time and breath. I bury my chin in my jacket and make myself smaller. Two sleeping bums are less threatening than one who's awake. The last image my beating brain is able to comprehend from the screen is a close up of the progressive alteration and confrontation of men and Nature.

The heavy boots stop next to my seat.

Massive, vertical pipes of legs make them seem smaller than they are.

Under my squinting eyelids, just one image fills up the entire corner of my peripheral vision. Live close-up of a massive, hairy fist (propaganda posters cannot picture it), loosely burdened by a scarred baton, hanging down from a leather strip around a protruding wrist. I swear now I can hear how atoms exchange electrons while forming molecules of chemical liquids, spelling despair under my bristled skin.

The stale stench of old garlic and fusty sweat.

Typical.

The watchdogs of all revolutions stink the same.

A hand sneaking from behind grabs my shoulder.

"Hey, you... Passport."

His voice chops the air with a bark.

The militiaman kicks me on the calf.

"Get up. Whoreson of a bitch."

An instant shattering blow. Pieces of glass pepper my neck. His heavy trunk buckles into my lap. Face down. Hatless. The uniformed fuck-head in a blowjob position. A streak of a bloody jam runs down from the base of his square skull. Marvelous... The piss-head is more dead than a deadbeat. What's next?

"Mighty strike, ah. He crumbled like a wheel-less bike." I free myself from the curled-up corpse.

M.C. is standing next to me like the center of the universe. Glittering eyes. Still holding the neck of the broken bottle.

Another meaty blow on the right side of the neck. The jagged top of the bottle is planted into the carotid artery.

"The unchanging ferment of repetitive historical change that emanates from the stinking stiff of this marginal, hopelessly philistine piece of shit... has finally reached the ultimate organic development in his enforced sublimination." M.C. scratches his nose.

"Drat... for every one of *those* who die, I feel way better." He blows air at his fingertips. "You better take a hike. I gotta beat the bear of my growing hair... but that's not the best I say."

And he is gone.

Well... the film will be over any moment now. But *now* is a very different 'now' from all the 'nows' I have experienced. Last night, I didn't help the German fuck-head to his death... the bloody still life on the floor is calling for action and not words. Run... but where? Outside... don't be stupid. They'll catch me in no time. There is no more outside. Gotta go in... under... above... trapped like a fucking rat. Rat... cockroach... I wish. There is just this door, half-open... back there. It gives me the heebie-jeebies. There...a crowd of uprooted soldiers, workers and peasants is streaming against me. A railway, a freight train, open carriages swarming with broken people and banners... and children... barefoot fucking children are running alongside the train... Like moths. As if they really wanna join the fucked-up gang of dead souls in the carriages. Give 'em daggers... and I run against them. I wanna jump into the screen and disappear there in the sea of grimy heads...

"Psss-s-st... Hey. Hurry... over here..." A voice from under the proscenium. "Get the fuck in here."

POSTLUDE

She said you can't have a
spine unless your book is
more than 130 pages. I
thought, spineless doesn't
sound promising. I
scratched my lower back,
sore from tennis but
spineful. "We only print
spine text on books with
more than 130 pages,"
she said. That's right,
that's what *she* said. *"We"*
– she said. Didn't she? So,
she must be one of them.
It's nokay to have no
spine I think. It's okay to

be spineless, but it's nokay to have a spineless book. A book is like a hook. Spineless hook . . . huh. Even my notebooks are spineful. I like their supple, healthy little spines, so durable. Women like . . . A notebook is more of a hook than a book. A notebook has more hook than a hook. So much hookiness inside a notebook, oh boy. The look of a notebook whispers volumes.

Sometimes it speaks more than the contents.

Ah . . . the forest of words inside. The atavistic world down below the surface of the words' subversive faces, the atavistic life encapsulated in the words' omnipotent roots. Oh boy . . . I really miss my toy. Books are different sorts of hooks. There is more meat to hooks and notebooks. Most books are meatless. I am no vegetarian. Yesterday she boiled a headless hen. Not the one who said that *"they"* don't print spine text on books with less than 130 pages. The one who boiled a headless hen, who feeds me well and treats me swell is my only muse. She takes a lot of adolescent abuse. (An unabused muse is not a muse.) I don't know who *"they"* are but I know for sure that *"they"* deal with gravity quite differently than I do. And how not... that's the most important plot. Or not... *They* seem so high and hot on any sort of plot. The merging of meanings doesn't support the majority of unshattered feelings. The merging of meanings castigates, castrates, most feelings, the Poet said before he puked in his sweat-drenched bed. (My silver pen just died like a well-staged sigh after an impulsive lie.) Always I do the same thing with those short-lived buddies of mine, no matter what color they contain in their straightforward guts. I

throw them behind my
back in a small waste bin,
four and a half meters
from my couch. Ouch . . . I
missed it. I hate to miss.
When I miss I hiss,
something in my mother
tongue, which of course is
not English and sings in a
different alphabet. The
expression I hiss refers to
the mother of some
unknown man, a stranger,
and more specifically to
the vulva of her genitalia.
Every time I deliver my
automatic hiss I get quite
perplexed and somehow

relieved by my vocalized verbal abstraction in spite of the explicit and concrete adjectives I pepper the air with. In fact, I hate repeating myself and always try to hiss unused, unabused ones. All goes. Let the pendulum swing. Though you can't stretch a ruptured muscle because it's ruptured. How many ruptured muscles will it take me to learn that there is no random drift of circumstances. For instance, an unusual murder (or was it self-defense?) sends the protagonist on a circuitous and unwanted journey punctuated by black (dark blue if you will) humor and vivid sexual suspense, mapping the road to an unexpected finale.

Huh...

All spines become fallen signs before the cruel judgment of killing time. Period. All spines are programmed hierograms.

All spines are peridial and
heavily   liable   to
periodicity. All spines are
signs   and   signs   are
signifying spines. (Wow!)
It is a great complexity,
but let me simplify (not
that anyone cares!). All
signs being made of time
are by subsequent crimes
against the integrity of
spines. Surely all spines
are betrayed by time's
despicable   relentless
crimes. Spines and signs
don't rhyme by random
drift of circumstances.
Spines deteriorate like

beams in coalmines. Do I

need to address the issue

deep down to the tissue . .

. or should I gently press

the   wrinkles   on   my

scarlet fez? Oh boy . . .

Eating,   drinking,

copulating, shitting, the

cycle of the circle is

closing squarely and now

in the name of my book's

spine I must try to outline

and designate the rate of

how my verbal bate will

turn imperceptibly into a

useless sign completely

undermined under the

frozen gegenschein up

there and down here
where an endless
saturnine vespine
coastline outlines the
waistline of this growing
fear dragging down the
road like a wounded deer
. . . It's all about the
fucking fear dear. It's all
about the atavistic world
just below the surface of
your fretful face. Like a
shark gone bone-blood
thirsty on the surfer's
shitful mammalian gut . . .
Can't be serious, the Poet
said seriously. An English
horn-sized black cat

pushed past him. He narrows his eyes at her. He looks at her as if she had had a big bosom explosion. I mean huge tits. I can hear a low growl. I bet the cat knows what he's been thinking. Precisely the way this Kaputev guy knew what *I* was thinking. By the way, don't ask, don't tell, but this name Kaputev is quite metaphorical. Now, don't get too euphorical about it. First learn what it means and then decide how to react. But please

don't *Google*. You won't
find out. If you *Google* a
bugle you might get some
frugal results, but of
course this won't be the
case if you *Googled*
Kaputev. It means
condom. Preferably, a
used one. Of course, of
course, my horse is off the
course and of course it's
one thing to have been
using the same used
condom, over and over
again (in those times,
contraception was sparse,
a rare item behind the
Iron Curtain) and quite a

different matter to use the very same condom over and over but in the full knowledge that the condom has been perforated for quite some time. And that's not fiction. Got it? Most likely not. Humor is like a tumor. It grows where it belongs. Unlike humans. Those are outrageous. Their humor is imitative. Tumor and humor are not contagious. Laughter is. Laughter mostly comes after. Like a tumor. Once it has established its

tumorous   ground.
Laughter follows, tiptoes
after humor's tumorous
nature. The Poet looked
at me and cried, you see,
humor   is   like   an
inoperable tumor. With
tears in his lower lids he
pointed at the painting's
bare tits.   So sad, he
looked like a freshly
castigated, then castrated,
ill-humored pet. Oh boy, I
wish he had his toy . . . He
works   his   breath   up
slowly.   Tears lap and
soak his eyes.   Then he
sighs. So fucking tired of

the lies. It's never wrong. That's why it's mostly considered wrong. It's 4.04. He seems to crave a wilted whore. The Poet is the guy who used to walk with a leg of ham on his shoulder and used to whistle his self-made tune about the fate of a very pale but male raccoon. Of course he did this tune in order to suppress his growing gloom and too, to entertain his lovely, precious cat. But now he's got his face like broken lace in his hands.

His flattened voice performs a shaky muted dance (as if he suffers from chronic reflux) into his palms. He says, you see, the wisdom of some books equals the usefulness of all hooks. Then shakes his fountainhead and mutters low. What a boring drama, this unending childhood drama. This persistent, so insistent size of mother's delightful cozy tits, spraying milk into my infant eyes, trying to obscure all sharp edges of the sky . . . The Poet and my precious Muse don't mind the infiltration of my abuse. So different they. The Poet is sometimes like a broken toilet. He leaks unfiltered wisdom, which basically is an understandable way to keep his mind going in certain preferred destinations. His voice is a warm-up tool for his scribing. His voice filters the unfiltered truths and often enough reminds him how not to scribe, I think. The threadbare state of his vocal cords delivered emergency services during these sneak attacks of palpable depression. I think. That's not what *he* thinks. He blames his intrauterine memories. I think he is a lucky man. He thinks he is unlucky and mostly miserable. He said his virtue of alphabetizing asserted his weakness by remaining an ungrown child, which at the end is his major strength. It's 4.06 (four o'six). My mind needs a

good remix. Having a
mind inside the mind one
shouldn't mind, I say. The
Poet put it more
poetically – his poems
write him out of his own
life. Every line is a
destination. It equals new
frustration at the station
of the lurking plot against
the plot, against life's
plotful pot. Think rot . . .
All plots, life itself, the
essence of myself, the
fucked up presence of
yourself, all start and end
in rot. I mean the plot of
rot is a fucking rotten

deal. I'd rather have the
brain of a baby seal and
drill the frozen waves,
raked light, the
ghostliness of sharky
waters, the spooky
melancholy of the fjords,
the haunting austere
drama of some stark
saxicoline panorama . . .
yes, fatful baby seal, away
from distant instances
and instant but distinct
influences, swimming in
the stream of the moment
like a blubbery sandwich
towards the beginning of
my ending, towards this

unforgiving, imminent encroachment of the waiting jaws. He said and went to bed. How sad . . . Though I must not forget that every written page is a cage but inside the page's cage there is an open stage. Bounded, grounded with the page this circular or square cage is usually in the center of the village fair where . . . its presence is entangled with absence. Nonsense. To pat a baby loaf of Irish soda bread is to prepare the pulpy tenderness of bloody gums for some salivating encounters. Though getting high on bread shouldn't interfere with the responsibilities toward the dead tree and the thing called me.

It has been not only in the past but also in the now that life predominantly is about some petty accumulations and not so pleasurable ejaculations. And how not? Messlessness *is* *not* emptiness. If any script is a verbal pit where shit happens, then messlessness is a border, an island where order has killed the joy of being. *"The joy of killing"*, the Joker seriously observed. The Joker is of course a poker and looks like one. He's got plenty in his locker. A soccer ball plus a glossy picture of a pussy hole. As fuzzy as a tennis ball. The Joker's truths are spare and austere. His eyes have been pecked out as a result of a practical joke. The Joker

24

is a different sort of talker. Poker face, but dressed like Johnny Walker. He never talks while he walks. His silent wisdom rocks. The Joker knows everyone's secret and I'm not joking. His rancid jokes are like my stenchy socks but luckily unmended, unlike my socks. I love my socks. I loved Lucy's reddish locks too. Oh boy . . . What a fleshful toy she was. She really took my high-pressured hose to a different level. I mean she even employed her little nose to rub the bursting body of my hose. She couldn't care less about messlessness, messiness or messfulness. Her quite messless life did not promote any particular interest in the subject of messiness. But the same can't be said about the Poet. Messiness is not a vice, he shared. Messiness is to be shared, he said. Messlessness, he went on, had been practiced by plenty of bipeds, not without pride.

Messlessness is like your Turkish fez. (He pointed with his greenish finger at my face.) It designates, appoints its carrier with quite specific beliefs and a vast spectrum of restrictions.

Messlessness, he says, is like restlessness . . . restless. Restlessness is in its bestlessness happilessness.

Happilessnessly speaking we are all quite unhappy but those who strive for messlessness seem to experience happilessness to the second power. Of course, their unhappiness is well powdered under a multitude of well-intended and defended reasons and a sea of reasonable doubts. The roundabouts of their messed up minds are incurably cluttered with uncluttering procedures. He might have said, decluttering activities. And how not? The plot of being is like the act of seeing. Super-mega-messy. The super-mega-messiness of life's

incorrigible hive is mostly
like a stinky, dinky, funky-
monkey dive. Life is like a
steaming piss . . . He said,
she has hissed in his hairy
ear. Either you can use it
as a disinfectant, a part
time sort of protector, or
you just drown in it like a
wounded, totally
misplaced defector. Feels
so good in the
neighborhood of a bloody,
broody, mood . . .

Re-minders. Never wear
underwear while you
scribe. Never use your

reproductive tool to reproduce. Never be a breeding tool. Let your piston-tool hang loose and cool. Use your horny piston with the devastating skills of Sonny Liston. Let its bulbous, brainless head stay ahead of other thoughts. Let it spill its primal flow every time you catch a female doe. The text is like your sex. Can't cheat the gear of your sex and fear. (Typical l'ogovism.) The text is like a post-coital or

perambulatory walk in
front flexor. To spill the
raw   sexol'ogorhythmic
vibes and treat the eyes
like hairy ears and twist
the seething power of the
mind, confined but free
behind   the   barred
window frame with a
view upon no view of
gluey hues. Stop rhyming,
man . . . How not . . .
Rhyming is like dining.
Hungry bastard, for this
foreign tongue. Lungful
stew of verbal hues. . . mh
. . . mh . . . m-m-m . . ., how
about the sexy clatter of

their high heeled leather
hooves. So attuned to the
bloody   agonies   of
broad—range   juicy
pussies brined in misty
sweetness, softly dripping
. . . trickling . . . Stop it.

Suppurating   and
infectious . . . Stop it!

Yet, yet, yet . . . let it be as
free   as   wanton
carelessness in the light of
the pale moon night (or
fright if you will). Man oh
man the moon tonight is
more than bright. Muted

rage . . . As pale-plain as
the anatomy of an empty
page. Inscribed profile of
the rounded lunar cage . . .
so caged, inside this
starry boundless cage the
Poet calls a universal
burst of cosmic spangled
purse.

Aa-aaa. . . can't hide
beyond the hedge of
percolating text, delivered
undivided in the darkest
hue of blue. Wow, how
cool, all hedges that
protect the sky's
illuminated edges tonight

are fucking high. Don't cry. It's only 10.05. Don't cry. It's still just 10.05. Don't cry. Just try to deconstruct your sadness into . . . the Muse's voice is trembling slightly like a mist on the hood of a purring Rolls Royce mood. I know, she said, the fists of your tristesse cannot be washed by the sliding nature of my words, but see, this furry ball of life was meant to flee you sooner or later. Let the dust come down. I know you think her beauty won't fade away, will stay and punish you for always. Painful starkness and the bleak mater-of-factness, the rupture of your casual logic, the essence of your fungi-ridden socks, the limping language of your mind, your stunned heap of brain, your refusal, your disapproval, the inventory of this shitty life-laboratory, the flimsy luggage of those tyrannies, will merge with the dreadful deed of her disappearance like a shattered walnut shell. Her missing hiss will spell the bell of hell, and how not, you have already been folded into a knot of grief, beyond belief, you need relief right now or else you'll end up as a dried-up leaf, or a rotten chunk of human beef . . . She uttered softly and asymptomatically.

Not enough grapes for her consolation wine. Nothing will ever be enough. Nothing will ever be enough. Nothing can possibly be anything, because it's nothing. And more so, *nothing* cannot possibly be enough or not enough whatsoever, because it is *nothing.*

Nothing looks like no thing. Nothing will never look like something. How refreshing.

Zippo

Nada

Nishto

Oh, nothing. . .

Oh, you preambular, prebiological command to *something.*

Oh, you just predetermined vacuum, pre-existent thing, which certainly was not a thing, or anything but sheer nothingness, preface of my face, facing me right now with your damn pop-eyed, obnoxious nothingness. Goggle-eyed, damn random nothingness, the Poet said to the Joker, but the latter just shook his sweaty head and went ahead.

Why mom, why . . . You fished me out and pulled me into something out there, away from my so comfortable nothingness, my ultra-neutral numbness, and drastically delivered me together with my helmeted head into this shitful puddle of existence. Through much resistance on my part, you delivered me with a caul and they of course

did not have a sterile
scalpel and punched the
suffocating   membrane
with rusty scissors (the
nurse used it mostly to
cut puzzles out of the
newspaper). They freed
my cauled head but for
this   successful   slight
delay I now must pay not
only through the nose but
also through my horny
pelvic hose, for the
consistent struggle for all
these seasons to go back
into your womb and
dissolve myself there to
my pre-existent state of

non-being. . . (so soon you will, the Poet gave me a reminder).

Oh mom, why me . . . Why did you make a life-pictogram of me. A diagram of me you hatched under your diaphragm, it grew into an artist, so all of them can think, oh yeah . . . another fucked up fartist. (No fucking fiction – nor blatantly dishonest non-fiction.) Oh mom, how come you conceived your precious son with a hooded helmet-head and now he's doomed to paint himself in a multitude of harnessed, hooded, muzzled heads of an essensualistic leper . . . Oh mom, it hurts my mental ham to jam my preferential thoughts persistently into pre-Freudian, prefigured nasty plots. But, was it the caul or was it the pressure assault on the soft skull? (One out of 80,000 comes with a caul.) Whatever the reason, the consequences are quite alarming.

Rhyming, crying, lots of flying, constant dying, et cetera. . . Though some old woman told my mom that I will be a very lucky man. Oh man, if I am lucky, the rest of humanity must be in a truly shitty situation. In a state of levitation I must keep my longhand flow, shedding words like rising dough and protect the letters' passive lassitude of whole wheat flour, white dust must of ground meanings . . . Dust eats ink. Dust eats

everything. Dust eats me.
Dust is like lust. Lustful,
dust is. Books turn
quickly into dustful
creatures. Book spines
and spines in general
deteriorate consistently
at an incorrigible rate.
Smaller books with
smaller spines tend to
deal with gravity's
merciless drill way better
than big and brick-like
books with fatful looks,
the Poet said before he
went mad (considerably
mad).

Did I mention that the Poet could be quite a joker on a given day while walking in the hay? Don't remember, but he, the Poet, loved to dismember his memorable past before he went mad. Before he went real gone, the Poet said that in his lyrical tendencies the Joker has been, is, more inclined to *incidents* than the Poet and with that way more poetic than the Poet himself. *No use to review your preview.* The Poet said. You see, he said, the view upon your own preview will germinate (to germinate means to deteriorate. Ripeness is already a sign of decay and decay is death's sort of preview say.) in Prussian-blue review of viewless point of view. But don't preserve the pleasure of your verbal gestures, sealed in a jar for aesthetic catastrophes. Some of those might turn prophetic, though you'll never know. And right there his iPhone barked like a wounded bitch. His left eyebrow twitched. He looked down with a malicious frown and yawned and then he read the following text: *"I only know what I want to know."* The Poet looked at me and spat like a shadow on a shooting spree. He spat like a rat decapitated on the track. You see . . . you see. . . , the fucking Joker is a fucked up mental poker. And then the last thing he said was, I am going mad. I think it's never bad to go completely mad before you go to bed. It's a well—placed, well-timed action of reaction as common as those repetitive *lexil'ogocontrac ctions* I have experienced for quite a while.

Faster, faster . . . You my precious, most contagious brooder, time is an adversary, the Number One intruder. *Faster.* . . You, my bitter Master, though I'm definitely no Margarita, you know. . . *Faster,* dive, headfirst

upon this imminent
disaster. Upon this
new *nextextflex* with no
pretext like early morning
sex. My muse interfused
the misty blues of dewy
air like *pain-thing* within
a painting. Don't let the
ox in the lucerne! She
blew me a kiss. Don't
little our little fox witness
an ox-explosion. Her fox's
risibility amounts to zero
possibility. She said. She
meant her ability to laugh
is zero, in spite of the fact
that her puss looks
laughterful. Faster . . . She

said. You've always been
heading, driving, diving
towards . . . imminent
disaster. Use your magic
word, you coined among a
bunch   of
naughty *l'ogovisms,* don't
delay to cut the hay of
home-grown letters and
then let them germinate
and grow into the open
field out there where all
belong and die, inside this
rotten pie called life,
where all belong and
crow the same old song
about the roundabout
where everything has

been squared in advance, where everyone is simulating someone else. No real intensities out there. Repetitive and boring village fair on the square. Mutilated egos barking loud at reality's broken back. Insentient bitch. Look . . . You can't avoid the void. You understand, you are a one-man band, the leader and the slave of your verisimilitude. A feeder. A hooded man by birth, lonesome leper, that's why I am your muse.

Need to be amused by you
and totally abused by
your super-ego-radar but
most of all often to be
bruised by your pumping-
piston-avatar . . . in my
oyster-like, briny-pussy-
jar.

She pulls down my smelly
socks. Jeeeez, your fungal
toe looks really puffed,
raw a pussful. She licks it
and gives it a mild suck.
My other foot (Dr. Derma
said, *"Show me your
feets!"*). I wish it had a
mouth, it slides down her

supple spine. I rub the groove of her back with the cracked, rough part of my hoof. Her eyes smiling, her mouth moves. Her wavy hair spills onto my Turkish pillow. Amuse me. She hisses. Then . . . she takes her right white mitten off and cautiously fetches a hair from the tip of her tongue. Amuse my horny holes. Those open fuses, but don't forget my tender ears. I need to know what your *next-*

text-flex is all about. Don't

pout! Speak out.

Screamplay is a sort of

hardcore play, a text to

explore when you feel

you're down and low.

Sadly funny, hasten drill if

you will against my will.

You know well my will of

course is not to write but

bite the nipples of your

gorgeous tits though your

current position looks like

an opposition to my will.

I say.

Wow, quite a bite you are today. Though I understand I can even comprehend writing is a form of biting. Bite me, write me if you will, you known I'm always on the pill. She wiggles out of her tight jeans. What's that? Something is bulging inside her black bikini. Don't fret; it's a green zucchini. Hump-day-warm up as you know, sometimes even I can. She bites the end of it off and shoves the rest into a pocket of her

purple, leather vest. You
better faster spill the
beans! She unzips my
shorts and throws her left
leg over my left leg, then
she goes into a crouch,
resting her crotch on my
left thigh and starts
licking my mushy big toe.
Her

animinianimalistic bikini
sharply cuts through the
deepest crevices of her
peachy ass. It's her way
to play with me and make
me spill my next synopsis
faster because she knows
my tendencies to

56

complicate things. She is
the opposite of me. She
simplifies   everything.
That's   why   she
is *my* Muse.

Each scream insists on a
different steam. The law
of life demands the arrow
and   the   bow   of
omnipotent   death.
Cannot deny my text can't
lie   the   Eye   of   your
bemused,   amusing,
museful I. I sigh, so close
to   her   ass.   It   starts   to
tremble   up   and   down.
She   presses   her   crotch

onto my hairy thigh. She turns her face back to me.

"Go synopsize your *Screamplay* song. Release the steam, my boy. Be mean, be dark, be a lean machine. . . , be dirty, shirtless pest, but please keep your beaten Turkish fez on while you ejaculate your mind and grind and merge your fucked up words, those useless crippled birds with the sticky-steamy sperm of yours. I will let you drill my ass as fast as . . . an automatic dildo.

Licks her smudged
lipstick. Slaps her right
buttock, then giggles.
Don't ever hide your clear
tears. The trick is to be
sick, but not contagious.
Like most of *them.* A
billion proactive assholes
in the hindmost corner in
the neighborhood of utter
brood. Right there, your
undisinfected *I* will serve
well for the fertile soil of
some unboiled allusions.
She looks at my foot as if
it has a tongue and as if it
had licked her on the
nose. Adjectives like

bluesful, solemn and proud you must avoid anyway! She gives herself a sideways look at the huge aquarium wall. I'm not sure if she can find her own reflection there or she is looking for *something* *else.* She fidgets with the pillar of my full-blown driller. I mean she plays with it in her mittened hand. Oh my, this waiting cock of prickful form is mating with an upcoming storm. She starts to tap the erected neck of my pleasure stick right below the anal eye, slight rubbing it into her deepest groove. She squints. My broody boy, you are *my* piece of ass but is your memory a private goddess or an immodest judgment of the times? Her little paw goes for my only ball.

Oh, wounded dog, Argonaut in quest of fragile beauty, oh lucky dog you have me as an undulating object, you are so free that you can't even see how free you are. You sculpt the paint and paint the words, you draw the succinctness of the present moment. The essentials are your true credentials. . .(the way she handles my ball makes me think that her sexual experimentation is situational) . . ., and if that was not enough you let yourself be the master of your letters. Speaking of your letters you can do quite better. D'sex parts are boring, ugly, repetitive – don't serve your talent. You are not good at taking out. Think of what you take out as much as what you put in. You really don't edit yourself, and you should. Kill your darlings! But if you scribe for your sheer enjoyment..., then fuck it, why bother. Luckily you have no brother. Oh boy, you've been quite complicated, different type of toy. Her spine wiggles under my fingers. Her backbone is supple and soft. Her milky skin, so white, so thin . . .

though I wish she didn't
oversuck my sick, mushy
toe and instead just gave
me head, a head of her
persistent lovemaking
wisdom. She looks
squarely at me, behind
her elevated peach
behind. A nice, succulent
blowy, I gave you
yesterday. But every day
is not Easter you know.
Just go ahead and spill the
seeds of your synopsis.
But short and to the point,
please.

Reclined on my back, I
read out loud...

An unusual murder (or
was it self-defense?)
sends the protagonist on
a circuitous and
unwanted journey
punctuated by black
humor and vivid sexual
suspense, mapping
(moping?) the road to an
unexpected finale. Right.
I read this but the drifts of
memory's wind bring to
my mind Lucy with her so
tight and juicy pussy. I
keep reading. Bogoman, a

failed film director, a total crossout pushed into a bout of self-defense with an elderly woman who accidentally shoots herself, is forced to quit his lethargic lifestyle and take radical steps . . . Oh my, just the sight of Lucy's pussy made me hike the rocky mountains of my priapic erections. However. Bogoman sends his girlfriend Berthe away to Vegas, dressed as the dead old lady in order to gain time and believable alibi, while his Russian friend, Igor, helps him deposit the dismembered corpse at a pig farm owned by a Russian Mafioso, which is a cover for necrophilia services. Oh my, how could I possibly forget Lucy's firm, lean, gorgeous udders, bouncy, super-rounded trouble-titty-rubbers . . .

. . . on the plane to Vegas, Berthe (not Gerthe!) meets an eccentric millionaire (is he a billionaire?), Shatty

Dumpmaster III, who invites her to his super-tacky mansion. Meanwhile, Bogoman shoots his first independent feature film with the help of Igor and Gerthe, the younger sister of Berthe. Bogoman persuades Gerthe to participate in the long pornographic opening scene as his sexual partner. Unexpectedly, in the middle of the action. . .

Oh my, I mean Lucy's mean and tiny waist and

the salty taste, down there, her orgasmic, sticky body waste . . . I mean so much juice and pussy-touch, contracting vise-like vulva clutch. How juicy was the whole of Lucy. Oh boy, how fuckable and chewy toy . . . she was.

. . . no news is heard from Berthe in Vegas. Gerthe is angry at her sister Berthe.

Hey, don't stop, don't stop, you horny, dirty rat! My gorgeous Muse has already impaled her peach-caboose on my probing healer-driller. Keep rocking me on your flesh-greedy, seedy, prickful bat. Pump me harder, deeper, steeper . . . The bedazzlement of her perspiring and pushing ass, like a hot-wet glove has trapped my busy tool and bangs it with no remorse of course. I reach and knead the kernel of her bloody clit. My left palm goes for her left tit and milks the traveling locality of her desire. Her ass begins to smell like a burning tire. Dissemination of her horny fire...

... oh boy, your tool has grown and hardened into a raging bull, drooling and designed to stretch my tissues and a truckload of overdressed and unaddressed mental issues. Faster, faster . . . fat-cocked bastard . . .

I festinate with one foot in the blues.

Last night, seized by that unspeakable hour of her prominent desire, she said while scratching my head that being a scriptor is like being an operator. Either way, she said, one has to be dedicated to an alignment, based fuck because one is constantly out of luck. Figuratively speaking, it's all about fucking and sucking. Happy men don't go to war. Most of them of course are lacking fucking and sucking because they are busy working, breeding and feeding. So many unfucked men and women. It's tragic. That's why history is tragic. She said. But you . . . oh boy, you are so fucking spoiled, scratched, fucked, sucked, fed in freshly-ironed sheets in a quite big and comfy bed . . . once things come to a boil, you pout, you shout, you lick some bloody clit of lovely tit or both, you go through hypochondriac fit. I've made you into a total unapologetic monster, big

time spoildy bonster. I
know how much you like
hot pepper sauce and
other spices, your fucked
up cause is out of place . . .
the flow and flaws of
paint and pains, remains. .
. Oh yes, yes, yes, you hit
the spot. . . Right on . . . go
on, go on. I know . . . I
know you've been a
brooding   leper
perpetually prepossessed
by the uncertain fate of
fading, upcast letters.
No? Yes? You know . . .
you'll never know! The
history of hopes is like a

history of rotten ropes.
(*Nice*). Ambidextrous
glistening of liberatory
dopes. (*You like that.*)
But see. . ., the crowd is
vigorously stout and
loud. All you have to do is
scribe stories and keep
them close to the spine of
your naked mind. Like
bones, she said, sticking
out of a fish's spine. She
said and scratched her
pussy red.

D'crowd is vigorously
stout and loud. D'crowd
experience no doubt. The
crowd is open mouth no

doubt. The crowd is always going South. The crowd is like a blood-drowned hound, spineless snake, a salivating snout wrapped up in flags and rags. The crowd demands to be deceived into a slut-finicky-submission, like a naked butt against a full-blown erection, like a dully and rusty cleaver, the crowd is craving to deliver. Don't go too near, the crowd survives on sour beer and the same old fear. The crowd is vicious lout, no doubt my dear, the crowd is a dying monument of untamed fear. Baleful, downcast abacus of flattened lives finicking against death's broadly open gate, constantly dissolving into buffetings of time and change. And no one gives a hoot about the wisdom of some books that equal the usefulness of all the hooks. (I hate repeating myself and if I do, I pity myself to d'core of my sore mental pit. It is nokay. But when my Muse repeats *me*, that's o.k.)

You smell like sea salt malt. She said, and whispered to herself, the lighter the body, the more durable the spine. The crowd is like a pit for bad affairs. The crowd is like a dried up tit of a hardcore whore. They tweet away the same old song. So long and legless and abominably boring is their only song, just stay away. Don't ever take part in their brainwashed, shitty play. Don't ever zig or zag while *they* zigzag.

Oh boy, some try to zag
while all the rest are
zigging and most of
course are slowly
drowning deep in their
zigzag runny shit.

Ayuh, she cries like a
distant harbor. Impales
her muscle deeper . . . to
be mentioned as a
pornographer is way
better than to be
remembered as a
biographer or a
choreographer . . . she
sighs. Ayuh, she cries
upon the dried up skies

and borrows hasten
service from my flipper to
her fine and smiley clitor.

I know you say
why *me,* why *you* should
kill this tree and flee the
stage of life with mini-
spiny book like this.
Why *me,* you say, should
scribe those postlude,
semi-obligatory pages,
why *me,* you say, should
spill lifelong and raging
fear in order to create
some order at the border
of disorder. Why? Empty,
unmoved faces, limp

through time with zero
traces. Fading, silent
pages soiled with rolling
rhymes, muzzled, utterly
confined and stuck in the
quicksand muck of
present times, like worn
out signs and sighs and
lies and literally dying
cries. . . , why *me.* Why
should I swim the sea
of *me,* right now and cut
the hay and pay the
wholesale fee.

Why *me?* Why *me*

and *I,* she said I said,

together with *my* Eye,

why *we* must tell the tale

about the alfalfa's rotten

bale.   She   said.

Why *I* together

with *my* bloody Eye, must

roll the verse against this

freezing universe of busy-

empty darkness, she said

I   have   said.   Why?

Why, *I* should   lie   my

troubled   Eye.   .   ,

because *my* lust for empty

space is a chronic must.

Why? Could it be because

I   really   need   to

reinforce *my* singing

order   inside   reality's

disorder? She said I have

said   and   then   I   have

added, she said, an antithetical one, after I had uttered *disorder.* And why the fuck must I be the man to mourn this fallen tree because of *me.* You see, the man who killed this tree is definitely *me,* she said I have said, with postlude attitude for useless, dying words like crippled birds, she said I have clarified. To scribe postlude is to prescribe a certitude upon persistent . . . *artitude,* she said. I've tossed *my* l'ogovism as a

platitude of sheer
l'ogovision. Surely
postlude is not exactly
necessary as a prelude to
another long, bone-like,
an ashful song
called *Artitude.* She said,
she has reminded me.
And please remember,
she scratched the nipple
of her tit, don't you ever
try to finish or complete
the inborn, horny anger of
your scribing fit. The
altitude of my
conspicuous brickbat will
dog you like a hungry rat.

But you must know that

this is not all, at all . . .

And this is not the best I

say.   She   said.

A NOTE ABOUT THE AUTHOR

Orlin G. Oroschakoff was born in Sofia, Bulgaria in 1952.

He's still alive.

For more biographical information visit ogoart.com